BOOKS BY THE AUTHOR

LITERARY ADULT FICTION
An Inventory of Abandoned Things (chapbook), Split/Lip Press, April 2021
Miranda (novella in short stories), Storylandia!, April 2018
Three on the Bank (novella), Storylandia!, July 2014
Cairo in White (novel), Musa Publishing, February 2014

YOUNG ADULT FICTION

Robin and Her Misfits (novel), Three Rooms Press 2023
Tink and Wendy (novel), Three Rooms Press 2021

WOMEN'S FICTION
The Troublemakers (novel), Black Rose Writing, August 2015

POETRY
I Have Conversations with You In My Dreams (poetry book), Alabaster Leaves, January 2016
Robots on the Horizon (poetry and prose chapbook), CreateSpace, July 2014

ANTHOLOGIES (Editor)
The Way to My Heart: An Anthology of Food-Related Romance (Fiction and Poetry), CreateSpace, August 2017
Candlesticks and Daggers: An Anthology of Mixed-Genre Mysteries (Fiction and Poetry), CreateSpace, December 2016
Unrequited: Love Poems about Inanimate Objects (Poetry), CreateSpace, June 2016
Dear Robot: An Anthology of Epistolary Science Fiction (Fiction), CreatesSpace, November 2015
Answers I'll Accept (Nonfiction), CreateSpace, March 2014

WEAVER

Kelly Ann Jacobson

Livingston Press
University of West Alabama

ISBN 13: trade paper 978-1-60489-363-2
ISBN 13: e-book 978-1-60489-364-9

Library of Congress Control Number: 2023939861

Typesetting and page layout: Joe Taylor
Proofreading: Annsley Johnsey, Angela Brooke Barger, Savannah Beams,
Kaitlyn Clark, Tricia Taylor

Cover design: Gracen Deerman

WEAVER

Thank you to Professor Ravi Howard, the Chair of my dissertation committee at Florida State University, for helping me craft my vision of these worlds, and for teaching me so much about the craft of points of view during my years there. You are the kind of professor I aspire to be. Thank you to the rest of my committee--Professor Mark Winegardner, Professor Elizabeth Stuckey-French, and Dr. Colleen Ganley--for your support. And finally, thank you to Joe Taylor, Director at Livingston Press, for supporting my book and giving it a home among so many great works, and to the wonderful editors there who helped with this novel: Joe Worthy, Cal Stephens, Summer Chadwick, Annsley Johnsey, Charles Thomas, Brooke Barger, and Tricia Taylor.

List of Characters in Order of Appearance — by Species

Laffians/Adalaffians

Sonamin	Mansel farmer, friend of Tamalin
Tamalin	First weaver on Adalaffa, first Laffian to make human contact, husband* of Moramin
Kamalan	Leader of the Elders on Adalaffa
Samiloon	Husband* of Kamalan
Moramin	Most skilled engineer on Adalaffa, weaver, wife* of Tamalin
Merrilin, Esq.	Defendant in the *Humans for Humans v. United States* case
Bren	Twin child of Tamalin and Moramin, member of "The Three Tams"
Ven	Twin child of Tamalin and Moramin, member of "The Three Tams"
Sig	Youngest child of Tamalin and Moramin, member of "The Three Tams," friend to Bina, later the General of the Adalaffian army
Deeklin	First Laffian taken aboard *The Santa Clara*
Brayadin	Mother* of Bina, member of the work crew of "The Three Tams," dies tragically
Bina	Daughter* of Brayadin, friend of Sig, aunt* of Sashan
Doctor Janamin	Council's advisor on the human body and founder of The HoFeLaffian Society for the Acknowledgement of the Lesser Species
Sashan	Fashion designer, partner to JoJo, student of Professor Agi

Note: These identifiers are the result of the human translator.

HoFe

Joh the Elder	"The Curator," compiler of the Virtual Exhibit on the Special Committee's investigation
General Fah	Leader of the HoFe Army
Mr. Lee Blain ("Lep")	Victim in Report Zeta
Mallora	HoFe child whose diary about being bullied is later used in the investigation
Professor Agi	Professor of HoFeLaffian-Human Relations, Elder at the Laffian arrival on HoFe, cousin to General Fah, husband of Sora
Sora	Healer, wife of Agi
Aduna the Red	Mentioned in *Elder Tales: HoFeLaffian Lessons for Human Children*, discoverer of hofellium

Humans

Pastor Felix Cantor	Leader of the "Humans for Humans" Movement
Officer Oliver Jones	Human officer in Report Zeta
Mr. Grant, Esq.	Prosecutor in the *Humans for Humans v. United States* case
Ruth MacMillner	Author of the article "One Man's Fight Against an Invasion"
Joe Williams	Founder of the Williams Rehab Center
Captain Rose	Captain of *The Santa Clara*
First Mate Adin	First Mate to Captain Rose on *The Santa Clara*
Doctor Braun	Doctor on *The Santa Clara*

Justin Belore	Inheritor of Belore Diamonds and Founder of HealthCorp
Lia	Child whose story was captured in the TV special "Arrival Day"
Uncle Barney	Lia's uncle, greeter on "Arrival Day"
Tanner Coleman	Assistant to Anna Belore
Anna Belore	Daughter of Justin Belore, CEO of HealthCorp
JoJo	Child of a human Den in California, partner of Sashan, student of Professor Agi
Father Jeffrey	Former priest, friend to General Sig

Curator's Note

When I was first asked to compile the evidence of the Special Committee's investigation for a virtual exhibit, I was hesitant. I am, after all, a member of one of the concerned parties, and though I was born on HoFe, Earth has become my true home. I started a pollution cleanup business here; I was elected to the Council of Elders here. I have neighbors, and friends, and colleagues here. How could I accurately reflect their struggle to pick which species would stay on Earth?

As I began the process of curating this exhibit, however, the selection and ordering of evidence occurred quite naturally. Partially this was helped by the number of documents thrown out due to their falsification—mostly on the humans' side—and partially by my determination to create, for each viewer, the experience of seeing both sides as equally valid. As I read these interrogations and articles and pronouncements, I did not envy the Special Council, and I understood why they deliberated for so long. In fact, I came to believe that neither side deserved to stay—that we should all be swallowed up by an earthquake and leave this planet to its more innocent creatures—and my pessimism earned me the Council nickname Jaded Joh. Perhaps you've seen the t-shirts on my constituents.

Anyway, a decision was made, and this exhibit is one old HoFeLaffian's attempt to reproduce the series of deliberations that occurred in the closed chambers of the Special Council. There will be others, I'm sure. Still, I hope that this official site helps give some context to the Council's decision, and that it brings its viewers some peace.

Long Laffa,

Joh the Elder

ARTICLE ONE

Official Order for the Formation of the Special Council

September 1, 2130

This is a sad day—a day that we, the members of the Council of HoFeLaffian Elders, had hoped would never come. We had hoped that peace would prevail—that *laffa*, which has come to be synonymous with your word *life*, would prevail—but the evidence speaks to the contrary. Everywhere, fires are burning. Everywhere, HoFeLaffians are dying. Everywhere, humans mourn at the graves of their lost loved ones and plan their revenge. Speeches are made; attacks are planned. We go on, and the battle goes on, and peace seems like an impossibility.

Since the beginning, there has been an ongoing call by HoFeLaffian politicians to make a firm decision about the matter of the HoFeLaffian occupation of Earth and its repercussions for the human occupants, especially in light of the humans' behavior since our arrival. Human interest groups have also expressed concern about the violation of HoFeLaffian beliefs by their new leaders, and about the HoFeLaffian rights to Earth in general.

We had hoped for peace—yet perhaps we were naïve. Because of our hesitation, chaos reigned. Because of our hesitation, laffa was lost.

A decision must now be made.

Yet we cannot be hasty. This is a complex matter, and one that requires intense study and deliberation. Thus, as of today, September 1, 2130, a Special Council of HoFeLaffian Elders has been created to gather evidence and hear testimony in this matter. Both sides—the HoFeLaffians and the Humans—will also submit evidence through a team of five representatives chosen by popular election. We want your voices heard.

By the end of this investigation, we will decide, by viewing key documents and hearing from witnesses who experienced different parts of our history, whether the HoFeLaffians or Humans will leave Earth for good.

You can read more as this investigation unfolds by going to www.HFLvHUMANS.gov.

ARTICLE TWO

Transcript of the "Humans for Humans" Speech

Delivered by Pastor Felix Canter

October 15, 2127

I want to begin today with a quote from Matthew 24: 4-6: "Jesus answered: 'Watch out that no one deceives you. For many will come in my name, claiming 'I am the Messiah,' and will deceive many. You will hear of wars and rumors of wars, but see to it that you are not alarmed. Such things must happen, but the end is still to come.'"

Let me tell you, people of God: We have been deceived.

You see, the HoFeLaffians are the pivotal deceivers. They came in their stolen spaceship and then waged and won a war we never knew we were fighting. By the time we figured it out, we had already given these deceivers everything: our homes, our jobs, and even our humanity. Why? Because these foreign adversaries convinced us to feel bad for them? Oh, how terrible, that HealthCorp found their wasting planets and gave them a way off of them—through fair labor, by the way, as is noted in Health-Corp's public records. How tragic.

It is not our fault that the HoFeLaffians decided to take a shortcut.

We should not pay the price for their idleness.

Yet we do pay the price, every day. Our people have become servants to these deceivers; the ones that refuse to bend the knee must beg on the streets for a few quarters. Yes, that's right, the best of us go hungry at night, and in the winter, we huddle around a fire and warm our hands and pray to God to deliver us from these cruel masters.

But do not be alarmed.

The end is still to come.

Those of you who know your Bible verses know what comes next in Matthew: "Nation will rise against nation, and kingdom against kingdom. There will be famines and earthquakes in various places. All these are the beginning of birth pains."

Birth pains, because with every act of uprising, we come closer to rebirth.

Birth pains, because soon we will be free.

Some of you already know what I'm talking about.

Some of you wait for nightfall and steal back what was stolen. Guns. Homes. You strike at these deceivers and reveal their lies, especially their claim that they believe in life—what they call *laffa*—more than anything.

What about *our* lives?

Thus we will bring the earthquake of our fury upon these creatures, and we will take back the kingdom that is ours. As Samuel says, "the Lord will not abandon his people." We have not been abandoned, my fellow humans, for God is with us, and He will make sure we triumph over the plague of HoFeLaffian rule. We need merely to rise up, and we will be guided to victory.

So I, Pastor Felix Canter, say to the HoFeLaffians who are on their way to arrest me: "Let my people go." Let us go, you so-called life-loving, honorable beasts, for these are the signs of the end of times—of your times—and with your annihilation, we will be reborn.

ARTICLE THREE

TRANSCRIPT OF GENERAL FAH'S RADIO TRANSMISSIONS
EARTH DAY THREE

Stand down; we are in control. I repeat, stand down; we are in control. Preserve laffa. Preserve laffa!

ARTICLE FOUR

From the Diary of Sonamin, Entry #455

Planet: Laffa

Discovered and Translated by Emily Marger

A few days ago the mansel trees put out their fat white buds and blossomed, and this morning I pulled my first mansel from its thorn cover like a baby's wet head guided out of its mother. Ten pounds, I thought, shifting the weight between my palms. Ten quillins, to trade for ten seed bags—or perhaps a sefer like Tamalin's to add fresh milk to my table.

"Look at this," I said to Tamalin when I passed their door. They whistled at the mansel in my satchel.

"At least nine quillins," they said.

"Ten," I corrected.

"Like it matters," they said, as though a quillin couldn't make the difference between a row of tomato plants or an empty garden edge.

Then I noticed they were dressed in the blue uniform of the Laffian Space Program. "Going to work?" I asked.

"Obviously," they said, pushing their shoulders back.

When Tamalin first got the uniform, they had complained about the color. *Aren't we already blue enough?* they grumbled as they spun around for the benefit of nosy neighbors. *That's the point,* I countered, resisting the urge to plaster my laffaberry jam and toast onto their chest. *The uniform is a symbol of our people—the first thing a discovered species might see upon arrival.* Tamalin had laughed me away, but I noticed they never mentioned the generic color again.

"And where is your work, again?" I asked. "The mud pits?"

"You know very well." Tamalin stepped out of their cottage to kick up dust and rocks in my direction.

"Watch out, or I'll kick back and ruin your perfect little uniform."

Tamalin retreated into the darkness of their cottage, and I kept walking. Is a perfect LSP entrance exam score and special notice of the General really cause for such arrogance? Then again, I suppose I would feel the same if I was singled out as a genius from a planet of herders and farmers.

Laffa.

Yet I couldn't quite accept it. I missed the old Tamalin—the one who had invited me, an orphan, into their pack of siblings. The one who threw me into the lake, and snuck me into their room to play flack-flack, and never told anyone about the time they found me sleeping on my mother's grave well after her funeral season ended.

I missed my friend.

And soon enough, they might couple and change again, this time into birth parent or parent mate with a new body and a new life…

Or maybe not.

After all, Tamalin seemed incapable of caring for anyone but themselves.

After I got home, I bedded the mansel in a baby basket and shook the pollen off my picking coat. The right arm had a bloodstain on the shoulder, and sure enough, I inspected the skin beneath to find the wound weeping white puss like streaks of storm clouds against a blue sky. *Quick, Sonamin*, I thought, realizing too late that my eyesight was darkening into an early evening haze. The poultice was across the room. I took one heavy step, and a second, and then my knees bent and felled me like a diseased mansel tree.

This is how I die, I noted with ambivalence, the poison having already numbed any regret emitting from my medial orbitofrontal cortex. With egotistical Tamalin as the last face I will ever see.

No. I forced my mind back, to a memory of lying in bed with my mother's hair brushing against my cheeks as she leaned down to kiss me. She smelled like laffaberries and the slightly sulfurous scent that always lingered on the other side of the mountain. The braid of red string she dyed with the berries and now wore around her head came closer and filled my vision like a sunset on the horizon. Funny, that little act of vanity to distinguish her from the other pickers—from the other Laffian adults in general—which did not at all fit in with her idea of a harmonious Laffa. She was complicated, my mother. I loved her.

And I love Tamalin.

I shook my head, but my vision of them would not clear. Focus on the laffaberry smell, I told myself, or on the red braid. Focus on the way she used to whisper *Long laffa, flower of my heart,* and how even after she left the room, I heard her echo until I fell asleep.

Wait.

The real Tamalin stood over me.

"Where's the poultice?" Tamalin yelled at me, though their voice was a weak echo by the time I processed the words. "Where, for laffa's sake? Can you hear me?"

"Yellow. Basket."

Tamalin disappeared and then appeared again with the basket, made by their mother for mine the year before she died, that held the titanium box with my precious items—the poultice, my mother's wedding necklace, and this diary—inside. They poured powder into their hand and spit, and then used a finger to mix the two together. "Brace yourself," they said, and rubbed the mixture onto my wound.

Fire on my shoulder. I screamed.

"Be brave, my friend," Tamalin said, and they took my hand in theirs. I was so surprised I forgot all about the pain.

"Are we still friends, Tamalin?" I asked.

They dropped my hand. "Of course we are."

The burning subsided into a dull ache. Mansel poison works that way—either kills you quickly, or, if you treat the wound in time, leaves your system in minutes. When I could prop my body up with my arm, Tamalin helped me crawl to a low stool at the foot of my mother's chair. By the time I sat up, I felt entirely cured.

"Thanks for saving me."

"Why do you still pick mansel fruit, anyway?" they asked as they pulled the green blanket on the chair over my shoulders. "You could be more than just a farmer."

"Oh, Tamalin, you understand nothing." I took the edges of the blanket and wrapped myself up. "It's the farmers who are the lucky ones."

I thought they would leave then, but they sat in the other chair and asked, "What do you mean?"

"Do you have any idea how beautiful an orchard of mansel trees is in the early morning, when the leaves mirror the sun and the fruits pulse like large hearts in their thorny chests? There is no better example of laffa."

Tamalin shrugged off my romantic description. They had no interest in either laffa the concept or Laffa the planet—their mind was on the stars. "I have to get to my training class," they said. Apparently, the conversation was over.

"Wait." I stood up on unsteady legs and found my balance. "I wanted to show you something." I dug in my picking coat pocket for the falana flower I'd picked that morning. Its bright orange petals were a little wrinkled, but the beauty was still evident. A sweet honey smell filled the small room.

"A flower? You wanted to show me a flower?"

"It's a falana flower," I said, smoothing the petals.

"Sorry, Sonamin, but I'm really late, and I don't have time to—"

"A lava flower." I passed them the stem. "I've never even seen one, just heard stories about them from my grandmother. They only grow in volcanic soil, and only at unpredictable times. I thought that maybe you could mention to General—"

"I'm really late, Sonamin." Tamalin tossed the flower onto the table. "Tell me tonight, okay?"

"Okay," I said to their back. So much for friends.

The truth is that I've noticed a lot of weird things lately, like the early harvest of mansel fruit and the odd herding of the usually solitary wild sefers on the mountain. Their hair is balding in patches, and their beards are thin and stringy. There is also the birdcall, which is notable in its absence. Not once have I woken this week to their pleasant chirping. And now that I think about it, the man who sells taniroak eggs at the bend mentioned resorting to jarred product because the taniroaks had not spawned in three days. (Reminder to my future self: taniroak eggs taste like algae, and not in a good way.)

That's why I wanted to write down some notes today, though I got sidetracked by my story about Tamalin, as always. I can't shake this weird feeling I have...

But maybe it's nothing.

Maybe...

Sorry, I dropped my train of thought. My extra quill was jumping a little on the desk, and it distracted me. I wonder if a herd of sefer is coming down the road. Anyway, I was saying—

There was a loud sound just now. I wonder if it's a landslide? I'm going to put this diary back—

Oh, dear laffa.

ARTICLE FIVE

Police Report by Mr. Lee Blain, Née "Lep"

Curator's Note: This police report, transcribed five years after arrival, is important not due to its uniqueness—there are many such reports, and a random sampling from the period would yield similar testimonies—but rather due to its timing. This report, later termed Report Zeta, was the final of such reports submitted before the Council decided to fire all human officers from the force. As you can see from this example, the Council's initial insistence on a blended agency was not successful.

Case Number: 426793401

Date: November 29, 2130

Reporting Officer: Deputy Mak Laster

Incident: Hate Crime Category HFL1-3

At 0400, police were called to the scene of a suspected hate crime category HFL1-3 inflicted on Mr. Blain sometime between the hours of 0330 and 0400. (Note: We are waiting on street camera access to confirm the exact time at which this incident occurred, as well as its severity, before classifying this crime as a level 1, 2, or 3.)

When questioned, Mr. Blain could only ramble nonsense phrases. Police, assisted by our HoFe translator and the Laffian witnesses, managed to piece together that Mr. Blain was likely forced to take a cab after being spit on and tripped by random citizens, and that, during the ride, he was driven to meet a group of human vigilante fighters, at which point he was stabbed.

Here is Mr. Blain's statement:

Late night at the office. 0300. Glasses off. Rub.

Eyes red in the mirror. The feeling of a brain squeezed like a stress ball.

Time to go home.

Hungover feeling, that unique nausea at the pit of my stomach as I bend over to grab my leather bag.

Food? All day?

A slice of pizza the size of my face. Man with the scowl, not his son, the one with the baseball cap who asks if I need anything else. No napkins.

"Alien," someone says. "Murderer."

Shoulders into mine. A foot stretched like a divider. Spit, spit, spit.

Moon too white. Too big. Like a meteor.

My bag, heavy like a weight, heavy like a weapon.

"Cat," they call me. "Kitty cat."

Eyes on the moon. Eyes on the Walk Sign.

"Meow," they cry.

Yellow cab. Paw up. Please.

"In," the driver says. A beard. Coffee smell.

A cold window on my fur, then skin. Eyes closed. Home.

"Uptown, eh?" the driver asks. Scoff. Squeeze on the wheel. "Figures."

Traffic lights. Little moons. Slow down. Stop.

Silence.

Dark alley.

Wrong way.

"Where?" I ask.

Open door. Fingers in my fur. Tug. Rip.

"No!" I scream.

Masks. Red hair, brown hair, brown hair. A circle, a ceremony. Human knife, ugly. Artless waving. Stab.

Cold concrete.

Suit off. Bag gone. Wet.

Live mouse at my mouth, scratching.

"Hey. Hey!" Someone new. Why?

Feet slapping. Receding echoes.

A Laffian's blue eyes. Flashlight moon blinding. "...Okay? Can... hear me? Are you...? ...hospital."

Sirens.

More Laffians. "Ready? Lift."

Glide.

The moon above is not mine.

####
####

After recording his statement, I provided Mr. Blain with his case number and the revised version of "Hate Crimes: Prevention" and "Hate Crimes: Recovery." I also gave him the list of suggested counselors aggregated by our department last year, which he put in his pocket, along with the pamphlets.

It should be noted that I was not present at the initial questioning; I was called later, off the record, due to some disturbing behaviors by the human officers, in order to supervise their investigation. During my time on-site, Officer Oliver Jones, who was assigned to the case initially, made several blunders during our time with Mr. Blain, including, but not limited to, the following:

- ☐ Categorizing the crime as petty theft until corrected

- ☐ Asking whether Mr. Blain had prompted the crime, which violates Rule #46

- ☐ Suggesting Mr. Blain stay in his home at night, which also violates Rule #46

- ☐ Saying, in an angry tone of voice, "Of course seeing a rich HoFe makes them angry. What do you expect?" This statement violates both Rule #46 and Rule #47

Please note that Officer Oliver Jones has been assigned desk duty until further notice.

ARTICLE SIX

Tamalin's Interrogation

Curator's Note: This "interrogation" occurred during the year of arrival, 2125, and was taken over the course of two days; both days have been included in this exhibit. All later interrogations of Tamalin have been struck from the record due to their perceived unreliability. It is important to note that the interrogators were not actually given any time to speak—when they asked any questions, they were ignored and talked over by the prisoner. Their attempts at interruption have been removed.

Day One

For a year, all we knew was the sea. Warm like bath water, the mild waves tempted us to stick in a finger, a hand—to even, when we felt brave, immerse our faces, pale blue sailboats that ducked amidst the creatures we called *laffafish*, translated in your language to "fish of life." Situating our faces thus would aim our spears truer than the on-deck view competing with the deceptive shimmer of two suns—and yet we never immersed our bodies, which stayed safely on the roof of our ship, *LaffaLaffa*, life of life, which had carried us away from the planet Laffa as it died a quick and moltenous death. *LaffaLaffa*, the only island we knew, the land we then called home. Giver of life…but what kind of life was it to wake every morning in your bunk, musty sheets damp with humidity from the open air hatches, single metal plate and cup waiting in a mesh bag strung on your bedpost, roommate above you snoring through both their mouth and nose hole, and the noise of our new planet rocking, rocking, rocking us to death?

One year.

In that year, three Laffians disappeared into the sea. At first intentionally, their heads bobbing like our buoyed nets as they braved the unknown depths of the green terrain; then horrifically, as they screamed and fought against some unknown force that grasped their legs and hauled them under. Three Laffians, and then no more, for how could we spare even one life of only two hundred? Even those last two had been accidents against the direct orders of our leader, Kamalan, who mourned the loss of every single Laffian with the formal fifty-day funeral.

Wait, no, I misspoke when I said "accidents." I apologize, my translator seems to be recalibrating.

Ah yes, there is the correct word.

Suicides.

There had been others. An escape hatch. A suffocation. Our people are thoughtful, and they do not make messes others must clean up. We worship *laffa*, after all, and not in the selective way of humans. To us, all life is sacred.

Just imagine: several years in space, a year on a floating ship in the middle of an alien water planet, two hundred depressed Laffians, *and not a single murder*. Not even a petty crime. Just those who wanted to live, and those who wished to die.

You humans would have gone extinct.

My father was one of the Laffians who forced the sea to take his life. I should clarify, here, that my usage of the word "father" is due to translation, as is my use of your human pronouns; Laffians do not have fathers and mothers, but rather "birth parents" and "parent mates." Anyone can be a birth parent; anyone can be a parent mate. The coupling does produce a hormonal response, which alters us in similar ways to your human biology. We do not often change roles after selection, but such things have been known to happen, rarely, in times of population stress. During our time stuck on the makeshift island of *LaffaLaffa* after the destruction of our home world, twelve partners separated dwellings, and five of those individuals changed roles.

Right. My father.

He and I were the only two members of our family unit to survive

Laffa's destruction, due to our positions in the Laffian space program. We were on base when the first volcano erupted; we were two of the first two hundred rounded up like a school of fish and propelled into the ominous black water of space, where we could no longer feel heat on our faces or hear the explosions of erupted ash. The remaining left on a second ship, which perished when a highly pressurized rock hit its oxygen generator. I cannot express, in either your language or mine, the feeling I had as I watched that ship fall; I shall select the metaphor of your extinct eagle, the last of its kind, wing-wounded, soaring over your proud lands with nowhere to rest until, drained of blood, he falls to Earth in a final cloud of dust and bone and loose feathers. We on the first ship cried out in one voice, one scream, and sometimes when I closed my eyes at night I can still hear it echoing over the water of this doomed planet.

My father. My father.

He had never been in space. He was a creature of the land, and his job was to figure out a way to make Laffian flora thrive in the ship's greenhouse. Of course, at the time of the volcanoes, his workspace was a simulated greenhouse on Laffa, not the ship, and thus we left his life's work behind with the rest of our family. See him, not in the program's blue uniform, but in a blue coat dusted with pollen; see his dirty fingernails, the ink on his hands, the magnifying glass tied around his neck with a piece of hemp and swinging, swinging like a pendulum. See him screaming as his greenhouse burned along with the rest of the station, the rest of our species.

See me next to him, a child in an oversized uniform, until that point raised to be one of the first Laffians in space and now just another refugee from a dead planet.

Your psychologists Sigmund Freud and Carl Jung would call this a "complex."

In space, my father became an unformed clay figure. He moved rarely, stiffly, put on weight and something different than weight—something like gravity. This force pulled him down until I thought one day I would find the clay that was once my father in a puddle on the floor. His eyes still focused, but on an invisible horizon. I would call for him, and he would stare, and blink, and sometimes turn, and in his stupor, would call me by the names of my siblings. Or no names, nothing, a stranger in the bunk below him.

Others were worse. One spaced himself in an escape hatch. One suffocated.

My father fought himself all the way to our second planet, and then, on the fifteenth day, I turned from my lookout on top of the ship— for I was of age by then, still a child in Laffian terms but what you would call a young adult—and saw a head bobbing away to the mild rocking of the waves. My father, I knew, even though back then all Laffians had the same brown hair cut to the bottom of the ear, the same long neck, the same blue face. Remember, you humans brought the curse of personal style with you—but I am getting ahead of myself. My father, back in his blue lab coat, waving a knife with his free hand while the other paddled him afloat.

I did not call for him.

How can I describe what I felt as my father buoyed away from me? My father, my only living relative. The closest I can compare it to is the feeling I got when we landed on our second planet, after a long and terrible journey, only to discover that nothing would change.

This is to say, I understood him.

He went under, as the others had, but then he did something new. He emerged. Not paddling, not even alive, but floating, face-down, with what looked like green rope wiring him tight.

I waited for the unknown beasts to come for their meal, but no life disturbed the surface.

I waited for the fish to disintegrate his bloating flesh, but no little mouths feasted.

I waited, and waited, until my shift was up. The next watcher immediately called for the captain, who called for a medic, and soon the whole remaining population of Laffa was taking turns waiting for my father to float over to the ship. I stayed until my eyes burned, and then slept sitting up against the other side of the open hatch with a pipe digging into my back; yet still, when I awoke a few hours later, I could make out his body.

For ten days, my father was a vessel for that green rope.

On the eleventh day, he delivered it to me.

The watcher on duty helped me drag the body onto the ship, twice as heavy and even larger than I remembered. I was surprised to find that my father was still wearing his gardening gloves and gripped a knife in his hand, which the end of the green rope seemed to have tried to reach. "What is that stuff?" the watcher asked, but I ignored them and focused on peeling the gloves from my father's hands so that I could shield my own. Then I went to work on removing what I by then had identified as some form of seaweed. The stipe of the organism had claimed his legs. The float ended at his belt, where the blades took over in bundling his arms to his sides. There was no sign of a holdfast, but the rough end of the stipe near his feet indicated my father had used his knife to cut this off and free himself before the sea claimed him.

"Horrible," the watcher said. "I think I am going to be sick."

I was thinking hard. With all of the extra weight and his arms held against his sides, my father should have sunk to the bottom of the sea. Yet I observed that the number of air bladders on the plant was astounding, so many that I had thought its beveled surface to be flat. The minute the hold-fast had been released, up he had popped, like one of your balloons against a ceiling.

And if the plant could hold him up…

And if enough of them were strung together…

"Get Kamalan," I told the watcher, who was clutching their stomach near the side of the ship. "Now."

####

Kamalan climbed through the hatch wearing her blessing garb, a blue, knee-length coat embroidered with the moons of Laffa and reserved for the births of new Laffians. Only two since our trip began, and the first one dead three days later. Her husband, Samiloon, followed her. These were our elders, though back on Laffa they had been everyday citizens, more than twenty years away from running in the general elections. These were our elders, who knew as much about this strange planet as the baby they had just finished blessing.

Who, in that moment, knew less than me.

"Long laffa to you, Kamalan," I greeted my leader as I formed an uninterrupted circle with my pointer and thumb fingers.

"Long laffa, Tamalin." Kamalan replied. Her eyes were on the body of my father. "We are sorry for your loss."

Samiloon removed his wife's coat and turned it inside out, revealing the plain black underside of the blessing garb. One side, life; the other, death. As your people would say, "two sides of the same coin." Kamalan slipped her thin arms, frail from the shared burden of our people's malnutrition, back into the coat. The only moons were the dark circles under her eyes. Kamalan knelt by my father and, while moving the sign of life over the length of his body, recited the prayer for the dead. (An aside, here: my translator has used the word "prayer," but I want to note that Laffians do not pray to any God or higher being. Only to life, and that is less a prayer than a statement of fact. We are alive, and we are grateful.) She then began the recitations of the fifty laffas, and Samiloon and I joined in, increasing the volume of our voices with every start. The whole time, I could think of nothing but my news about the seaweed, but I channeled my enthusiasm into the laffas. Only when the last booming laffa left our mouths to drift, like my father, across the water, did I speak my mind.

"Leader Kamalan, as you know, my father worked in the Laffian greenhouse his whole life, and he knew more about plants than anyone. He taught me about the air bladders of seaweed, and the way they float their blades toward the surface to receive light for photosynthesis."

Kamalan and Samiloon nodded politely, but I felt their impatience. There were more Laffians to comfort, more rationing decisions to be made. Or maybe, they simply closed the door to their dwelling and lay, as I often did, in the warm water of their despair.

"What you might not know is that my mother was a basket weaver. An old art form, but one passed down through her family for sixteen generations."

More nodding. A glance exchanged.

"This was her knife." I pointed to the blade lying next to my father. "He used to borrow it for his work, citing that a weaver's knife is the sharpest on Laffa. As you know, weavers back on Laffa used heavy willow rods to create their masterpieces—"

"Tamalin," Kamalan interrupted gently, "I would ask you to remember that laffa is precious, and that—"

"—which got me thinking, why couldn't we weave very large baskets out of the seaweed on this planet to use as boats?" I rushed ahead. "That way we could explore our surroundings without using up the ship's emergency reserves."

Now their looks changed. We Laffians are a hopeful people—one who worships life must be trusting, in both its gifts and its miseries. You Earthians know that by now.

"You think that would work?" Kamalan asked.

"I do. The high number of air bladders would make a seaweed boat quite buoyant—enough to hold several Laffians inside."

The look on Kamalan and Samiloon's faces was one I recognized—the same look the admissions committee had bestowed on me as they granted me a spot in our planet's first space program. The look my mother had given me when, upon coming through the door of our cottage, I knelt at her feet and presented my new blue uniform.

The look that acknowledged that I was special.

And oh, how I wanted to be special. How I yearned for it, more than fresh water or a *mansel* (what you would probably call a type of apple, though on our planet they grew to the size of an Earthian melon and were shared between a family only on special holidays due to their rarity and thus expense). After Kamalan and Samiloon returned to their quarters to report to the other elders, I stayed next to the dead body of my father and day-dreamed—daydreamed!—about what the General of the Laffian Space Program would say when he heard about my discovery. Would he remember me? Would he recall my perfect LSP entrance exam score? Maybe I should have reminded Kamalan of my position, or bargained for a spot as a captain, or—

Idiot. Attention-seeking child, while his father rotted less than three feet away, his skin and bones and organs already deteriorating into pieces of that new and horrible planet.

I digress.

Once I remembered my father's body—and I admit it was the smell that interrupted my reverie, not a single kind thought—I put my mind to a burial. On Laffa, our dead found eternal sleep in their own yards, with no headstones or caskets to slow their journey to the beginning of the cycle of laffa. On this planet, the sea would do the work of digging, covering, and decomposing for me, so I decided to embrace the role of nature and push my father's body back off the boat. He was heavier this time—or perhaps the watcher who helped me drag him up had done more of the physical labor than I wanted to admit—and I grunted as I put my full weight against his shoulder. Water oozed into a puddle beneath him like a shadow. "Come on," I said, to myself or to my father, and then I gave him a hard shove and watched him disappear the same way I had pushed my older siblings off the dock behind our cottage into the lake. His face became a muddled reflection of mine and then nothing.

My father.

####

The elders approved my proposal. Since none of the other Laffians had any experience with artisan work—after all, they were what remained of our space program—I was put in charge of five mechanics and three physicists who had fished back on Laffa. The fisherman, as they became known now that physicists were essentially useless, would procure the seaweed using a dummy and a knife attached to a pole; the mechanics would weave those strings into boats with the adeptness of men and women accustomed to wire repair.

Or, at least, that was the plan.

My job, the most important of all and without which the mission would most definitely fail, was to teach the mechanics how to form a boat. The only problem? I had largely tuned out my mother's explanations about weaving, spending instead the late-night hours by the fire staring up at the stars and visualizing my first steps on a foreign planet. Sure, I had helped her gather the rigid rods, held them as she forced the soaked pieces into a base, but once her muscular arms began the work of threading the weavers up and down, up and down through the sticks spread like spokes of a wheel, I had rested my head on a pillow and gazed upward, toward the expanding universe.

Little had I known that the survival of our whole race would rest in those arms.

Of course, there were technical problems, too. We had no rigid rods to serve as stakes. Our fishing lines broke. One of our fishermen was pulled into the water by a seaweed strand not severed quickly enough, and though we saved him, the knife met his leg in the process. For the first two days, the suns beat against the deck of our ship and roasted us, so we took to working at night and sleeping during the day.

Yet our work continued.

At night, the waves lapped gentle at the hull, and we found ourselves weaving to the beat of their tongues. The planet's five moons played audience to our performance. One mechanic, Moramin, was the most skilled among us—if we had been an orchestra on your planet, they would have sat in the first chair. Every upward and downward motion of the seaweed was like a dance, a flirtation, as their coaxing fingers threaded the seaweed through the bent pipes we used in place of rigid rods. Often I found myself watching them instead of working, and until the weaver behind me bumped into my back, I forgot all about my new responsibilities, and my dead planet, and my father. Then I trudged on, until my arms and legs ached and I surrendered our troop of weavers to the enemy of exhaustion.

Eventually, I asked Moramin for a drink.

Our people had brought no alcohol with us from Laffa, but a skilled brewer had found a way to turn some of our harvested seaweed into what you humans call "gin." It says a great deal about our desperation that we turned the seaweed into an intoxicating substance first, and only afterward began experimenting with the plant as a soup stock, as a flavor for bread, and most recently, as a biofuel. We longed most to forget our current position, not survive it. Every night, the cafeteria filled with Laffians, and Moramin and I had to wait a half cycle—about forty minutes in Earth terms—before we found seats. I held up two fingers. The bartenders wore the flasks of gin around their necks for safekeeping as they hurried from table to table filling mugs.

"Salty," Moramin said as they gulped the gin.

"Like drinking our work," I replied.

Like toasting my father's death.

Unlike most Laffians, Moramin kept their chin-length hair in small braids, and as they talked, they tinkered with the braids, turning every word into a musical note. On Laffa, these braids had likely been secured by twine; on this planet, where all we had was our ship, they wrapped the ends of each strand with a small wire.

I liked the braids, but what I liked more was the fact that Moramin found themselves worthy of such a use of our limited supplies.

"More?" I asked.

Moramin held up their mug.

The salinity faded as our taste buds adjusted. I forgot about my father, about everything but Moramin. They told me about their family back on Laffa, and how they had ended up an apprentice to a mechanic five days before the eruption. Their mother had walked them to the station that day, but the two of them had been divided during the explosion. "I was the last person on this ship," they said, "and she was the first person on the second one." Down went another gulp of gin. "Lucky me."

The night wore on. The bartenders trudged slower and slower between their tables, and their eyelids began to droop. The suns had come up hours ago. Eventually, we all trickled out of the cafeteria as the first shift of servers arrived in their hairnets. Moramin and I paused at the fork between our hallways.

"What's your roommate like?" they asked.

"Dead."

They threaded their fingers, calloused from weaving, through mine. "Your place, then."

####

That night, I woke to the sound of wind through seefin vines—those beautiful epiphytes, garlanding our mansel trees in red; those slow killers, choking our mansels and precluding their fruit—and opened my eyes expecting home. Instead, I found Moramin, still asleep but muttering and tapping a message violently against my arm. "What is it?" I said, leaning on my arm so that I could place my ear by their mouth and listen. "What are you saying?"

"Landing legs—down. Engines—three down, three operational."

"Moramin, wake up—"

The tapping continued, faster now. "Temperature regulation—down. Bathroom suction—down. Heat shield—down. Total system failure, estimated—"

"Moramin!"

They slammed forward, like they were buckled in during a rough space dive. Their braids shook and clattered. Sweat caught the glow of the green safety light.

"Bad dream?"

They climbed out of bed. Watching them dress, I wondered if I was the cause for the hurry—if I was the mistake. Such thoughts rarely occurred to me then. Soon Moramin was a distant stranger in a standard uniform and tool belt. "I have to work," they said, an afterthought. A lie? "You understand."

"Sure." I had not moved. "Listen, if you don't want to do this again, I don't care—"

"Yes, you do." Moramin bent down and brushed their lips against my neck, the prelude to a kiss that never came. "Drinks tonight. We'll talk then."

####

For a few hours, Moramin was gone; then they were weaving at my shoulder, again part of our desperate machine. We did not speak, except to contribute to the general conversation: a debate about the benefits of mansel root in the case of upset stomach. I was doubtful; the others insisted. "My mother always gave us lake water mixed with brinklin," I defended. "That herb could heal all ills."

"Or just make you throw up until you forgot what ailed you," Moramin said, their first comment to me since that morning.

"You didn't like it?"

"Hated it." Moramin shuddered. "Fed it to the sefer whenever my dad wasn't looking."

That got a laugh. Whom among us had not fed our sefer some unsavory snack, whether it be brinklin or a hearty spoonful of bitter mashed blueroot shoveled between the sefer's curious lips?

"I liked the hairy texture." I could almost feel the thick leaves in my mouth, tickling the roof and sticking between my teeth. "And how my mother always said, as she cut it, that eating it would make me smarter."

"Guess she was wrong," Moramin said with a straight face. Then they smiled, a new expression for them, and I marveled.

So much for not caring.

That night, we got drinks again. This time, Moramin wore a necklace of woven wires beaded with a few clunky bolts.

"Nice necklace," I said.

They did not smile. "It's the dreams," they said. Then they motioned for a mug.

"What?"

"The reason I left this morning. I've been having these reoccurring dreams about the ship malfunctioning."

I waved my hand in a grand sweep. "In case you haven't noticed, the ship is already malfunctioning. Severely."

Moramin shook their head. The waiter filled the mug, and in one smooth motion, Moramin gulped down the gin and held the mug up for another. "I mean total systems failure. Not today, and not next year…but one day." They waved for another, gulped again.

"Our space program knew what we were doing." I was cocky. I was like a seaweed strand floating on the surface of their concern. "We built this ship to last for generations."

"Yeah—in space. You haven't seen the engine, Tamalin." More head shaking; the beads clinked their worry in rapid harmony. "All of this moisture and salt is slowly wearing down every single piece. The landscape of this ship is changing, and we don't have enough replacement parts to rebuild it. It's like watching a mountain wear away in the steady wind and trying to fix it with a few shovels full of dirt."

"But—"

"No." They turned their mug on its side, gesturing the end of our evening.

"Alright, then we'll make our boats and cross the water to find supplies," I said. I did not turn my mug. What was there back in my room? What was there anywhere but here?

Moramin shrugged. "We have to. But the odds that any living species on this planet has the right supplies to fix the ship… or even the materials to build those parts ourselves… Face it, Tamalin. We're stuck on this planet for good."

ARTICLE SEVEN

Excerpt from the Transcript of *Humans for Humans v. United States (2146)*

Curator's Note: The following court case details the legal proceedings of the groundbreaking 2146 case Humans for Humans v. United States. This case, in which the Humans for Humans group sued the HoFeLaffian government of the United States in an attempt to remove the newcomers from Earth, is known not for its results, which were as expected, but for being the last court case in which human law was followed. From this point on, the federal and state courts were disbanded in favor of a planet-wide elder system. However, its contents have proved very important to the Special Council's deliberations on the HoFeLaffian's presence on Earth and should be studied carefully.

Testimony and Notes of Evidence, taken in the above-entitled and -numbered case, before the HON. MARIA WILSON, Judge, presiding on the 15th day of June, 2146. APPEARANCES: REPRESENTING THE PROSECUTOR, HUMANS FOR HUMANS: THOMAS GRANT, ESQ and. REPRESENTING THE UNITED STATES: MERRILIN, ESQ.

MERRILIN: May this set of graphs recently presented at the HoFeLaffians' yearly gathering of elders be marked as Plaintiff's Exhibit A-D for identification?

MR. GRANT: Objection, these graphs are misleading because they were made as propaganda and portray the role of the HoFeLaffians on Earth as more positive than the bleak reality of their residence. My client, Humans for Humans—

MERRILIN: Actually, Your Honor, I think you will find that these graphs— which were created by a human sociologist, by the way—do nothing but give an accurate portrayal of the current situation of the physical and mental health of the HoFeLaffian people. Unlike the opposing counsel, my goal during this trial is to present all of the facts, not give partial evidence to garner a more desirable outcome.

THE COURT: Objection overruled.

Exhibit A:

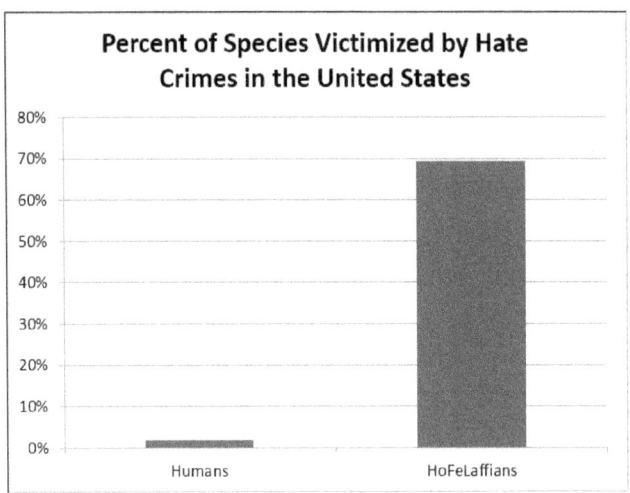

Exhibit B:

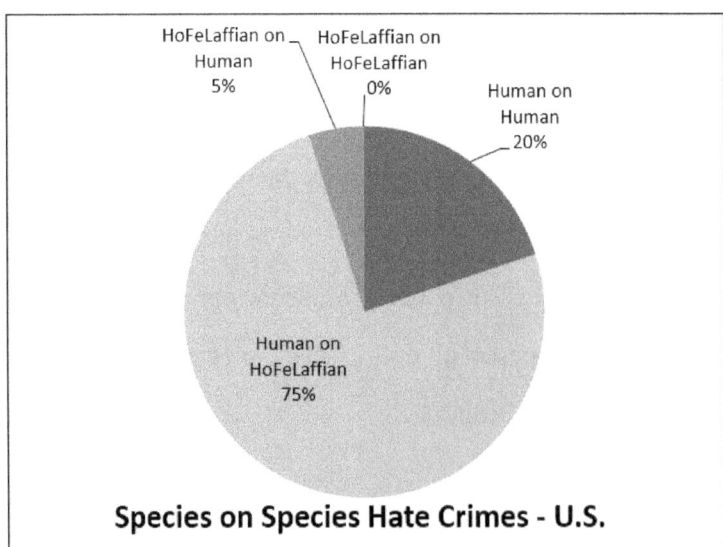

Exhibit C:

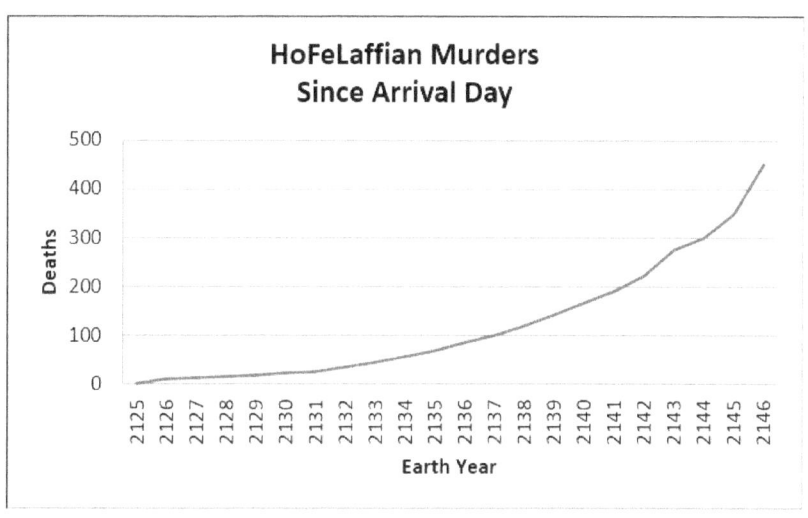

Exhibit D:

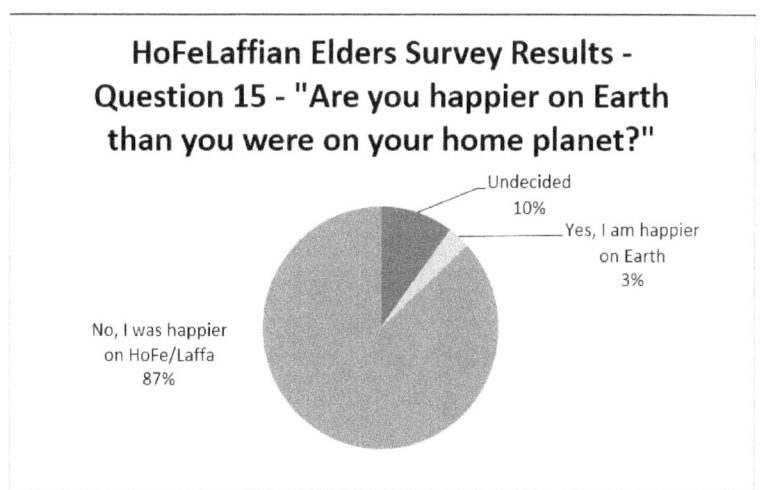

ARTICLE EIGHT

ONE MAN'S FIGHT AGAINST AN INVASION
by Ruth MacMillner
Après News Volume 12 No. 3, Year 2140

Thursday, I drive out of the city and into the dusty stretch of nothingness where farmers once plowed their fields. I see a few stragglers picking beans, pathetic crescents of blackened green, from their front gardens. One or two tip their hats. Hard to imagine this life, full of physical labor and subpar produce, when one is selecting the most perfect carton of berries at the local depot. Hard to imagine why anyone would stay a single hour more than they had to.

"This is home," says Joe Williams, who I have driven five and a half hours to meet. He sits in a rocking chair—or, rather, just the bottom half of one—and squeaks a calm beat on the old porch. The backrest has long broken off, but it still stands against the house, probably to be used for kindling.

I ask him what home can mean when everyone and everything he knew has packed up and left.

"Not everyone," he says. "We have our family here. A few neighbors. And our numbers are growing by the day—but that's why you're here, ain't it?"

I bring up the HoFeLaffians. I'll admit, I'm hoping for a few old-fashioned curses, maybe even a spit over the railing or some such outburst. Instead, Joe just shrugs. "They don't bother us. We don't bother them."

"But then why start Williams Rehab Center?"

Joe takes a deep breath. He is a small man, stripped to the bone and tough—like a lizard, I think, or a wild fox. His beard is a salt-and-pepper stubble, and his hair is stringy around his ears. He chews some unseen thing in his mouth—the end of a wheat stalk maybe, or good old-fashioned tobacco.

"People started coming here. First a few, then fifty, then more than we had houses for. Not good people—not people with their values in order, I mean. These people were angry. They had poison in their souls that no amount of preaching could suck out—and they were poisoning us too. One day I got to thinking: You know what these people need, Joe? They need to be saved. Not by God, but by good old-fashioned work. So there you go. That's the whole story."

But that is far from the whole story. Joe takes me down to the Center, a compound hidden behind a hill, which now houses four hundred small cottages. There is a mess hall, a lavatory, a meeting room, and a general store. "People trade," Joe explains of the store. "Seeing as they ain't got no money and all."

A few things are glaringly missing. Cars, for example—there is not a single vehicle, not even to take the people from their homes to the fields where they grow their food. Joe explains that cars are against the rules—if people bring them, they have to park them in a separate lot and leave them there unless absolutely necessary.

"Are there other rules?" I ask.

Joe shows me a sign with the commandments, as he calls them, handwritten out for all to see.

1. No lawbreaking.

2. No hateful language.

3. No mentioning the old ways unless you're in Session.

4. No vehicles, cell phones, or other pieces of tech nology.

5. If you want to eat, you have to work.

6. If you want to work, you have to follow the first five rules.

"Amazing the power of a square meal when people are starving," he muses.

And those people are everywhere, like ants in a farm. They carry baskets of beans, water jugs, flowers. They look dusty, tired, and sunburned, but they are happy.

"Amazing," I agree as I take in the scene. "But there must be people who ignore the rules."

Joe sighs deeply. "Oh yes. Those we run off, and they don't come back."

I wonder what he means by *run off*, but I don't ask. Guns are illegal now, and I don't want him to say something he'll regret, even to a black-market news reporter like me. Yes, I am nervous for him—me, the reporter who went undercover as an alien just to be able to write a descriptive piece on Laffian genitalia. That's the ultimate power of Joe: he's surprisingly likeable.

Joe walks me past one building labelled "S." This is where residents have their Sessions—which we, in the old days, called therapy.

"And this is a requirement?" I ask.

"Oh yes." Joe nods vigorously. "As I said, these people carry a lot of weight on their souls. Someone needs to help them lift it off." He leans in. "This is against Rule #3, but just between us folks, my mommy and daddy was just like them, back when the big company that I can't name first came around. Angry. They wanted to fight. They had jobs before—in the case of my mommy and daddy, a beautiful farm; in the case of the residents here, fancy jobs in law offices and news desks and such. We even have a neurosurgeon, if you can believe it. He cans the vegetables. That's what I realized…"

I lean in, too, so that I can smell bacon on his breath. "What, Joe?"

He surprises me by taking my hand and patting it, like I'm his grandchild or a loyal stray. "We're all the same, Ms. MacMillner," he says, continuing the slow patting. "Even those HoFe-Whats-Its. We just want food, water, and a place to call our own."

ARTICLE NINE

Transcript of Tamalin's Interrogation

Day Two

We made five boats before our first expedition. By the time that Kamalan selected the four elders, five physicists, a single cartographer, two mechanics, and two weavers—including myself, who was of less importance now that the rest of the weavers knew the trade—to accompany her across the water, Moramin had completed her physical transformation and was pregnant with our first child. I was only seventeen years old.

"I wish I could go with you," she said as she helped me down into the boat.

The floating discs were small—just wide enough for three people per craft, plus food supplies for two weeks and a tracking beacon—and rocked mildly in the waves. I barely noticed the motion, so desperate was I to begin pushing across the expanse of the sea with my makeshift paddle. Our plan was to go forward for a day, make a right turn and push on for another day, and then come back at an angle—unless we hit land, of course. Upon our return, we would set out again, and again, and again, until we had covered the immediate area. Then our path would lengthen. We knew only that the planet was smaller than Laffa—thus about half the size of your Mercury—and mostly comprised of ocean.

As we soon discovered, this initial assessment was accurate.

There is no land here.

There is no life besides fish and the algae species they eat.

There is no end to the great green sea.

####

I am not proud of what happened next.

"Tamalin?" Herlindin, the cartographer, had put their hand on my shoulder. I became aware of it. I felt its weight. Five fingers, like the grip of five seaweed strands dragging me under.

"No."

"We have to turn back—"

"No!" I wrenched my shoulder away. I was aware of the other voyagers pausing to look, but I was beyond shame. "There has to be something here. If we just keep paddling, we will eventually—"

The elder assigned to our vessel—I forget his name, now, though I cannot forget his face—tried to take my paddle. In my panic, I swung the oar like a baton. The sound of the flat end against the elder's face was like the low thud of a pot falling from my father's observation desk onto the floor. That, too, had been my fault. That, too, had been the result of my father, my loving father, telling me no. *Don't touch, Tamalin. These are for the ship.*

And much like the herbs growing in the clay bowl, the elder creased at the middle and fell, fell, fell, and as he fell, I watched him and felt vengeance. The seaweed was thick there, hungry. The elder was a scream, a blue face under water, a shadow.

"I'm so sorry," I lied to the water.

Mindalaffa.

To lie, literally translated as *To sin against life*.

But you know all about that, don't you?

####

Another year passed.

Another.

Another.

Time was like the blank space of the sky between when the suns disappeared behind the haze of the atmosphere and when the carousel moons rose in an easy chase.

With no choice but to accept our fate, our people finally named the planet: Adalaffa, or "after life." We drank gin and settled into a general malaise. When our clothes wore through, we wove new tunics from strands of divided seaweed, so that even our bodies became monochrome.

We might as well have been dead.

And yet, we could not die. In fact, despite our best attempts, we grew; our population was like the animal you call Tardigrade, or "water bears," which can even survive exposure to outer space and be reanimated.

Adalaffa.

During those years, Moramin and I were the first Laffians after the elders to earn our own boat. Though the voyages had been unsuccessful, we had still solved the problem of where our growing population of people would live, and every family who later tethered a rope to the *LaffaLaffa* attributed their freedom to us—to me.

Moramin was also the first woman to bear a child on such a vessel. "Laffa," she told me as she pressed my hand to her stomach, where I felt the hard ball of the uterus against my calloused palm. "Laffa," I repeated. And yet we both sat there for a long time looking out over the water in silence.

On the day she went into labor, my wife was in the middle of fishing for seaweed when she suddenly curled into a ball and screamed. "What is it?" I asked, but she could not speak, and her eyes looked beyond me.

"Get the doctor," I yelled across the water at the neighbors watching our spectacle. Finally, someone moved, a teen, and as they disappeared toward the ship I thanked laffa they were quick on their feet. Moramin screamed again, again, again, until her voice went hoarse and her face froze in wordless agony. Sweat dripped from her braids and wet the basket into a dark halo beneath her head. I tried to hold her hand, but she clawed me away like a wild beast.

After twenty long minutes, the doctor and his five physicians-in-training, all of whom were barely old enough to reproduce themselves, crossed the bridge to our home with the teen. "Stay back," the doctor told the eager trainees, who had tried to add their weight to our delicately balanced boat. "Observe, record, retain." The doctor had forgotten his lab coat, but luckily, I had a clean tunic for him to slip over his uniform. He put his hand to Moramin's stomach and then inside of her; she howled, and my own cervix clenched in sympathy. Moramin arched her back like a fish on the line, and one of the assistants had to help me hold her down so that the doctor could work the child down the canal.

"Even our own bodies have forgotten the joy of laffa," the doctor said as he shook his head. Yet as minutes turned into hours, and as the suns disappeared into the sea and became the ghostly moons, we knew this was something more than just a lack of laffa. Laffians labors should be brief and painless—my own birth was considered long at eighteen minutes—but Moramin's was a battle. She could not eat or drink, could not answer the doctor's questions, could not even say my name. Blood and excrement mingled on the basket, and repeatedly I washed them away.

Finally, in the light of the next morning's suns, the enormous child slid from her body into the doctor's arms.

"Are they ok—?" I started to ask, when another child, a rare twin, fell out onto the basket and rolled once before settling against the doctor's knee. We both looked down at the baby, but neither of us moved to pick it up. I looked at the first twin, then back to the second, then back to the first again.

Something else was wrong. Something had changed. "Doctor…?" I whispered. But he could not speak, and neither of us reacted when Moramin held out her hands for her children. Finally, with shaking hands, I lifted the second twin from the basket. As soon as Moramin saw them, she withdrew her hands.

The baby was green.

Seaweed green.

"Our species adapts," the doctor mused as he rubbed his thumb over the newly cleaned foreheads of our children. Then he looked at his hands, as though expecting the green color to have worn off. "I suppose this gift is what comes to the children of Iaffa."

Gift? I looked at my children, their alien faces the living embodiments of a planet I hated, and fought the urge to throw them into the water. Moramin looked away and did not stretch her hands out again. Of course, later she fed them, nestled them in baskets that rocked from the natural rhythm of the boat—laffa was still laffa—but neither of us said a word as we drifted to sleep on our mat. Neither of us felt even the semblance of love for those mewling babes who returned us to the sleepless nights of our weaving days, those captors who kept us servants to their survival.

Those children of Adalaffa.

####

A few weeks later, the doctor returned to inform us that it was the gin, that blessed drink, our only escape, that was responsible for this deed. "We are cursed," Moramin moaned, and I agreed.

And yet, we were soon forced to reconsider.

For every day that the Laffians wasted away, the vitamins divided between us not nearly enough to replenish the dwindling supply from our home planet, the twins grew stronger. Within a month, they were twice the size of a normal Laffian infant. By a year, they could have wrestled a five-year-old and won—not that their baby minds had any capacity for strategy, but you understand the point I am trying to make—and by three, we had to trade our boat for a larger model to keep from sinking. They had other gifts too, which we would only discover later: the light from the suns did not burn their skin, for example, and the seaweed would not touch them. They did not require the nutrients of Laffa, and thus drew all they needed from the fish, the seaweed, and the water.

They were our curse, Moramin and I, and yet they were the true salvation of our people.

My jealousy for the attention they received from the elders was almost overpowering. Moramin took her anger out on her hair, which she braided and unbraided with such vigor that I began finding brown strands on her pillow, in the morning gruel, and around the fingers of the twins. Another child came, of an even deeper green hue, and Moramin wept all night.

Like us, the rest of our people bred like animals, but there was no farmer to cull the herd. The linked boats became a village, and then a network of villages between which we constructed bridges that functioned like spokes leading back to the *LaffaLaffa*. Our engineer friends still on the ship told us that at night the empty rooms were so quiet they could hear the garbage disposal humming its slow churn.

Yet life on the boats was no easier. The seaweed disintegrated, meaning that our homes required constant upkeep to stay afloat. Whenever we were not fishing or cooking, we were inspecting the strands, rethreading them, and acquiring new strands by cutting the tendrils from the sea. Our eyes were always downcast, searching every step for signs of wear. Our shoulders hunched and our knees required constant soaking. Our hands stained and grew calloused; they were like the ink-marked hands of your artists, only we resented our work, and thus our hands, and thus ourselves.

Another year passed.

Another.

Another.

Kamalan died, and soon after, Samiloon. The next elders were re-placed, died, were replaced, all so much younger than the grayed and fading Laffians who had once led our people until the end of their two-hundred-year lifespan. Not that we needed them for much, when the most important decisions were how to allot the gin or where to build the next bridge—and to think, we had been a people with a space program.

We had been a people with pride.

Many nights I drank alone in the ship's cafeteria. Few Laffians now journeyed to the boat for their gin, preferring the recycled bottles of alcohol allotted to them every week over the cramped quarters of our former prison, but I came often, especially when Moramin drank my share too soon. I was given extra rations—for my role in our people's salvation, and for my position, Advisor to the Elders—which I hoarded from my spouse like one of your dragons sitting on their gold.

"A people with pride!" I repeated to my server, who seemed drunk himself by the way he kept leaning against the table's edge to pour.

"Pride," he agreed, and sloshed out extra into my mug. "Long laffa!"

I sighed and sat back in my chair. Long laffa. Was that even what I wanted? How many days of this incessant weaving could a being of higher sentience bear? Maybe I should follow my father into the water, I thought. Maybe I should steal enough bottles to drown myself in gin.

At some point, I must have trekked down the hallway toward my old quarters. Sometimes I slept there, in my father's old bunk, until the morning headache woke me. This time, however, I was halfway there when my heavy steps were diverted by a strange noise from the other direction of the fork, a kind of gurgle that was not water or garbage disposal or anything Laffian. I was drawn to it, that sound, as your moths are drawn to the bulb fires that fry their beautiful wings. What was it? Why was no one else investigating it? My feet plowed forward, until I reached the communications room where the transceiver that had received the dying message of the second spaceship had since lain dormant.

Where now, as I stared at the speaker with my mouth gaping, an unfamiliar voice in an unfamiliar language repeated the same unfamiliar words over and over again. To this day I do not know the words of that message, but I do know how I felt as I listened to it, the same way I had felt as I explained the air bladders to Kamalan.

Of great importance.

My vision was blurry, and the red button to open transmission appeared as two. My hand aimed, missed, tried again. There it was, cool metal in my palm. Down I pushed, silencing the words that had been repeating.

"Hello?"

I took my hand off the button and listened. A new voice answered, though in the same foreign language.

I pressed again.

"My name is Tamalin," I said, "Tamalin of Laffa. My people are stranded here. We need help."

"Tamalin," the voice repeated, and at the sound of my own name, I took a step back from the machine. "Tamalin, Tamalin, Tamalin."

I stepped forward and eagerly reiterated into my microphone, "Tamalin, yes, that's right. I am Tamalin." I would have kept talking—or likely repeating my own name, the selfish child that I still was—but suddenly the lurch of drunkenness felled me into the chair. I believe you humans call this situation "room spinning"? A strange term for a completely physiological occurrence…then again, I understand the desire to blame the internal on something outside of the self.

After all, I am the Laffian who fell asleep during the first communication with another species.

Yes, you heard that correctly.

I, the supposedly great Tamalin, first Laffian to contact human life, fell asleep on the desk while the voice on the other end sang its meaningless song.

In my dreams, I drifted, without direction, in the green seawater.

####

"Tamalin? Tamalin?"

The voice woke me. The tone was familiar, like a mother's on stirring a child, and the pronunciation was perfect. I know, now, that the spaceship's advanced translation software had taken over, and that for three hours the computer had puzzled over this new word, Tamalin, and finally termed it a proper noun. A name. Mine. And once Tamalin had been established, the journey to the sentence structure of the great "I am" was a quick one. From there, "My name is." From there, "Help." I have seen the report, and the complex codes, and the transcription of the dialogue happening on your explorers' bridge as their ship came closer to our planet and entered its orbit.

EARTH TIME: 0315.

LOCATION: IN ORBIT AROUND THE THIRD PLANET FROM THE SUNS IN GALAXY 12,542.

TRANSCRIPTION:

CAPTAIN ROSA: What do we know?

FIRST MATE ADIN: Not a lot, Captain. You know those scientists—their heads are so far up their asses that they're actually in their conference room examining the periodic table. Spoiler alert: it's H2O.

CAPTAIN ROSA: [Laughter] If we didn't have a responsibility to HealthCorp, I would space all five of them without hesitation.

FIRST MATE ADIN: Seconded. Anyway, we also put our guy Tuck on the readouts in case he can spot anything we can't, but he's an environmental control tech, not an alien expert. I doubt he'll come up with much. The Communications Systems Techs tell me they think they've cracked a name—Tama…Tama…I forget, it's Tama-Something—and that a name can be all they need to reach the grammatical structure underneath.

CAPTAIN ROSA: Has this Tama-Whatever said anything else since he went quiet an hour ago?

FIRST MATE ADIN: Not a peep.

CAPTAIN ROSA: Intriguing. [Long pause] Maybe this lifeform is more intelligent than we first believed.

My name was the key. My name, of which I was so proud, became a joke to you humans before you even met me. And how can I argue? I had the print of my tunic sleeve embedded in the dehydrated skin of my face. My back refused to straighten into an upright position. I was like one of your dragon legends hunched jealously over my treasured microphone—

and yet, I did so instinctively, for I had no memory of speaking into it the night before.

"Tamalin?"

I pressed the button. "Yes?"

"*Holaffa.*"

The computerized voice spoke in my own language, and yet the word was devoid of any emotion. Typically, the word *holaffa*, which roughly translates in English to "hello life," has a certain emphasis, a throwing open of a window and greeting a new day, that the computer could not imitate. Still, I understood the point.

"Holaffa," I repeated.

Footsteps came down the hallway. My shoulders tensed. "Papa?" a voice asked, and then one of the twins, Bren, appeared in the doorway. At least on the ship they had an outline; on our basket, with the dry green seaweed below them and the green water behind, they chameleoned into Adalaffa. Luckily, the seaweed did not attack them, for both twins, Bren and Ven, and the youngest, Sig, had accidentally been pushed overboard many times because we had not seen them.

Even their names, meaning literally First, Second, and Third, were barely identifiers.

"Papa is busy, Bren."

"But Papa." Bren looked down at their feet. "Mama says there is a ship in the sky, and she wants you to come see it."

####

The spaceship was a paused bullet. It hovered just low enough that I could see the markings on the right side—HealthCorp—though at the time those white lines were just scribbles. The rear of the ship shot a stream of exhaust in a blue tail far behind the engine. Its height did not waver—just close enough to see us, but not close enough to come into range of our rockets, had the *LaffaLaffa* even been capable of such maneuvers—and yet it did not depart.

"Where did it come from, Papa?" Bren asked. They leaned into my hip, and I fought the urge to shove them off.

"I don't know."

I found myself holding my breath. Minutes passed, then an hour. We know now from the public log that during this time Captain Rosa ordered the crew of *The Santa Clara* to scan our ship and the part of the planet they could see. We know that the humans very quickly surmised the ship's damage, our status as refugees, and our nonthreatening nature; we also know that their scientists determined Adalaffa capable of sustaining human life.

Yet they did not descend. They did not aid us.

After an hour, they slipped back behind the green haze of Adalaffa's atmosphere.

I sent Bren home and returned to the communications room. *"Holaffa?"* I asked the microphone in a pleading voice. *"Holaffa? Holaffa?"* No one answered.

I cannot explain the betrayal I felt at this almost-encounter. I had called this ship, conjured it like one of your magicians, and yet the rabbit had escaped my grasp. Imagine how my people would have loved me for bringing their savior. Imagine how every Laffian, now Adalaffian, would have thought of me with every solid step on dry land.

"Holaffa?"

Yet though I returned every night for a year and drunkenly reenacted my first encounter, the humans were long gone.

####

Since receiving access to your planet's history, I have read a great deal of conflicting research about the man named Christopher Columbus, whose ships—including *La Niña*, originally christened *The Santa Clara*—inspired the names of the HealthCorp fleet. Explorer. Colonizer. Religious crusader. Dreamer. Monster.

At one point, he even had a whole day named after him.

Yet many of your people hate him. Such multi-mindedness seems uniquely human. On Laffa we had elders, but they were loved by all or removed without protest. Our history was peaceful; we had never experienced the concept of war. Our slogan was, and had always been, "Unity in laffa."

I think a lot about Christopher Columbus now, and sometimes I even dream about him. I picture him as he appears in one of his supposed portraits: large and austere, with a black tricorn hat. In my dreams he descends from *The Santa Clara* like a god, and when he steps onto our baskets, they become puzzle pieces of a continent where our crops can grow. He teaches us the human methods of cultivation, and their architectural designs, and their words. He cultivates and designs us, too; we begin to look like him, white and tall like the twins, and our hair turns pale.

At the end of the dream, we always drown in a wave of green water.

####

"This is not Laffa, Tamalin."

Moramin sat beside me on the mat. It was early morning, and I had just come in from a long night at the microphone. My vision was blurry, but I could make out her outline, the helmet of her braids, against the flashes of sunlight that came through the woven roof of our hut.

"Let's talk about this tomorrow." My eyes shut.

"No," Moramin said. She shook my shoulder until I opened my eyes again. "Now. I doubt you've noticed, but we have another child on the way, and none of the others are big enough to mend the boat without supervision. I need your help."

"But the ship—"

"Is gone." She took my hand. "You spend all of your time looking for answers in the sky, but the truth is already clear: whoever spoke to you on the microphone did not want to help us."

She was right. I knew she was right. At another time I might have argued anyway, but my eyes itched, and my stomach churned, and I needed sleep. "I'll mend the boat." I rolled over to my other side, ending the conversation.

The next morning, after a shot of gin to ease my hangover, I put on a fresh tunic and went out to help Moramin. I had not noticed the way her belly had swelled, nor the widening of her hips, and as I watched her struggle to bend for a rotted strand, I felt like I was actually seeing her for the first time in months. My eyes had been on the sky, while right in front of me, Iaffa had continued its steady progress.

"Let me," I said as I reached for the knife, and she squeezed my arm in gratitude.

The strands bit into the skin of my softened hands. How long had it been since I put my own sweat into that boat? One by one I removed the old seaweed pieces and strung in new ones from our depleted pile, until the boat was a vibrant green. My children watched me from the door of the hut. Did this man at work seem like a stranger to them?

"Come," I said. They scampered to my side. "It's time you learned to collect the seaweed yourselves. Your mother and I will not always be around to help you."

The twins had grown taller since the ship, and though they were only seven, their heads almost reached my shoulder. Bren was round and shaped like a fish, while Ven was thin like seaweed. Two halves of one laffa, I thought. Yet I had to admit that I did not know them, not beyond what I could see; I vowed that I would try harder from that point forward.

I gave each twin a knife. Little Sig—though now not so little at my hip—wanted to learn too, so they were given the bread knife that had been part of my ship's standard utensil set. Bren held their knife like a dagger, while Ven held theirs like a pen.

After we tied the knives to poles, I placed one of the sharp poles in each child's left hand and one of the bait poles in their right. "Be ready," I told the children. I showed them the way to stand, with their legs apart and feet planted, and how to shift the pull of the seaweed so that they did not fall in. After they tentatively placed their poles out into the water, the frantic tugging of seaweed sent each twin swinging their knife pole. They brought in their catches, untangled the poles, and cast again.

"I got three," Bren soon announced.

"Well I got four," countered Ven. "I'll race you to ten."

Soon enough each twin had a pile of fresh seaweed so large Sig could hide under it. How many times had I hidden in my own mother's supplies, thinking that she could not see me just because my face was covered by stakes?

"That's enough," I announced. "Remember, the goal is always the promotion of laffa—laffa for all."

"Laffa for all," they repeated.

To make my point, I had each twin bring our neighbor, an elder, half of their catch. They were reluctant to let go of their prized collections, but I knew that they would grow accustomed to the Laffian way eventually.

"I like when you're here, Papa," Sig said while the twins were across the bridge.

"Me too, Sig."

When they returned, Bren and Ven brought a small allotment of seaweed jam in the bottom of a metal cup. "From the elder," they explained, and I marveled at the generous gift. Such a treat involved sugar, which was so precious we only received one tablespoon a month. Moramin was still resting, so I decided to teach them how to make Adalaffian bread to eat with the jam. Bren got the bag of dried seaweed, and Ven found the metal pot we used to make all our meals. "I want to dump it!" Sig cried. They spilled a little bit of seaweed on the boat, but most of the pieces went into the pot. Bren and Ven took turns crushing the pieces into small flakes we then combined with a hydrated yeast packet and previously boiled water from our water pot. I wondered, as Sig stirred, whether Moramin had picked up last month's yeast supply, and whether she knew how many packets remained on the ship. Not many, I knew—and how precious the lumpy dough in front of me seemed when I thought that I might never taste the heavy delicacy again.

"Long laffa, Tamalin," a voice yelled from somewhere in the distance, and I looked up to find a Laffian waving from three boats over. Did I know that friendly person? Had we met at the cafeteria late one night and exchanged stories, or had they retrieved our supplies for Moramin as I slept away the afternoon in my father's bunk? Or did every neighbor but me know the names of their fellow citizens, and me by process of elimination?

"Long laffa," I called back. Later, I decided, I would bring over what remained in our bottle of gin and greet them properly.

Returning to my work, I kneaded the bread with the children's help and then left it to rise under an old tunic while we rested on our mats in the hazy sunlight. Little Sig rested their head in the place between my arm and body, and Bren and Ven casually lay with their shoulder touching mine. "What a beautiful day," Ven said as they blinked slowly. I tried to imagine Adalaffa through the eyes of my children, to whom the hazy sky and the green blankness were their only home. "Beautiful," I repeated, not because I agreed, but because my wish for them was that they never know how much I hated this place that had made them.

"Look, Papa," said Sig, whose voice sounded suddenly very awake. "That ship is back again!"

They descended through the cloud cover like a lid over the pot of our cursed planet. Somewhere behind them, the sunlight reflected against the shine of their bullet bulks, but to us, the celestial bodies had disappeared completely. The sound of the engines was like the inside of a hurricane. Our boats rocked against the new waves their exhausts made, and I clutched my children to me to keep them from falling overboard. Moramin ran from the hut and called Sig to her, and I carefully handed him off so that she could secure him inside. The twins quaked against me. The ship, our salvation, was back—so why did we feel so afraid?

Here, I am tempted to ask you why you decided to bring a fleet for this first meeting. And yet I suspect I already know the answer, so I will continue with my testimony, for laffa is short, and we have many years to cover.

Regardless of motivation, you came with a fleet, and unlike the first ship, these ones hovered much closer to the water and then landed not far from my boat, on the very outskirts of our farthest village. From my view, I could see the outline of a hangar door emerge from the smooth hull. The door swung upward, and a ramp that led down to the water lapped out like a tongue. The first humans on Adalaffa stepped out.

They were so colorful.

So beautiful.

Not just their skin, but their hair, their clothes—and their eyes, their freckles, their shiny accessories later called "jewelry." Nothing about them resembled the unity of Laffa, or the dreary camouflage of Adalaffa, even with many of them in uniform. They stood on that ramp and looked down at us, and we marveled at them like statues in one of your museums.

Then, five boats down from mine, the Laffian closest to the ramp leapt over the few feet of water separating them from the ship and landed with a loud boom on the metal structure.

The humans stepped forward and put out their hands.

The ramp went up.

The outline of the door disappeared.

We were left staring at the reflection of our own forsaken planet in the hull.

####

"And what can we do?" one of the elders asked over the din of voices in the cafeteria. No boats near the human ship could hold our collective mass, so we had retreated to our own ship, though its emergency power supply offered no actual protection.

"My spouse is in that ship!" cried a Laffian. "Am I supposed to just leave him in there while those—those—" We had no Laffian word for alien at the time, though we have since adopted the English word.

"Creatures?" suggested a nearby Laffian.

"Right. Those creatures do…do…" We had no word for torture, either. "Do whatever they are going to do to him? What if he gets hurt? What if he dies?"

"He won't die," said another elder. "I am sure this has all been a misunderstanding, and as soon as the creatures determine that we are harmless, they will release your husband immediately."

Voices overpowered the elder. Moramin's mouth moved next to me, but I could not hear her. Usually Laffian meetings like these were calm, but the presence of the humans had already begun to shift something inside of us. My ears, accustomed now to silence, ached from the noise.

While the elders tried to make themselves heard, I slipped from the cafeteria and down the hallway into the communications room. After so many nights of attempts, the chair had the impression of my body, and three empty gin bottles littered the table. A fourth had a swig left, which I downed in a quick gulp. Then I sat and put my hand on the red button.

"Holaffa?"

Static came from the other end. Someone adjusted the frequency, and the static went away. *"Holaffa,"* repeated the computerized voice. *"Nona affada. Afen degiva lalaga Laffa."*

Do not be afraid.

Your friend is giving us the language of Laffa.

"Good. Can you tell me why you are here?"

"I must think." The computer paused for a long time. I heard voices, in an unfamiliar language, in the background. Finally, the computer spoke again, in a broken but clearly translatable sentence: "We are here for to save."

#####

Retalaffa: literally translated to "returned to life," but meaning "to save."

I think about this word often these days.

You see, "To rescue from harm" is your most common human usage for the word save, but ours is, "To save from drowning." The discrepancy makes sense, considering that Laffians rarely encountered harm on our home planet—especially not harm from other Laffians—but on Adalaffa, we encountered the possibility of drowning many times. The elders came up with that word, *retalaffa*, to convey the feeling of being dragged from the water and given new life.

When your computer passed on the message "*Retalaffa*," I thought that your ships had come to rescue us.

Wouldn't you?

However, we have another word that stems from *retalaffa*: the word *resalaffa*, which literally means "to sustain life." This is the word your computer should have used.

Resalaffa.

In common usage, it means seaweed.

####

An hour later, the humans informed me they would release the Laffian. I, in turn, told the elders, who had divided all of us into groups of eight per boat and sent us back across the bridges to our outskirt village. Laffians stood shoulder to shoulder across the diameter of each boat, forming one long greeting line, and waited impatiently for something to happen.

The door opened.

The ramp descended.

The Laffian who had leapt aboard, Deeklin, appeared looking much the same as when he had left. Same tunic, same bare feet, same brown hair, same dusty blue skin. I could not have picked him out of a crowd. And yet, something had changed, for he held his shoulders high and practically swaggered down the ramp toward the eager people pressing closer to the edges of their boats.

"Laffians," Deeklin announced with the authority of an elder, "these creatures are called humans, and they, too, are worshippers of laffa. They mean us no harm. In fact—" he motioned to his left, where a strange crane began to descend with a large box attached to the end, "—they have brought the people of Adalaffa a grand gift to celebrate this important meeting of our two species."

"A gift?" We marveled at this turn. Gifts were quite common

on Laffa, but they were not exchanged on any kind of holiday or special occasion. One might give a gift to a neighbor, like the seaweed that morning, or leave a flower on the pillow of one's spouse, but they were always unprompted and never used in direct exchange. Even our festival days were reserved for meditations on laffa, dancing, and food.

"What is it?" Moramin whispered to me as the box neared the surface of the water.

"I don't know."

A few inches from the water, the crane released the box, which weighed enough to make a wave that rocked every boat in its proximity. The crane deftly moved its claw to the top of the box, pulled some kind of lever there, and retreated. The walls of the box fell away, revealing a stack of large discs made of some kind of hard material I had never seen before. The best way that I can describe them now is to use the human concept of the Frisbee—or rather many enormous Frisbees piled on top for easy transport—but at the time, I thought they were one large storage silo.

"They are boats!" exclaimed Deeklin. He waved his arms in excitement. "The people of Adalaffa will never need to weave a strand of seaweed again!"

The bafflement of our people became excitement, and talk struck up on every vessel. After countless hours completing and repeating the same tedious work, had the humans really brought us such an easy solution?

What thoughtfulness!

What generosity!

I, however, said nothing. There was a bad feeling in my stomach worse than any hangover. After our communications an hour before, I had assumed you were there to rescue us—yet you presented these boat-like monstrosities, monstrosities that only made sense for a life on Adalaffa.

Why?

"Oh, and one more thing." Deeklin seemed to scan the crowd. "Is Tamalin here?" Over a hundred pairs of identical eyes turned on me. "The humans requested to speak to him personally."

####
####

The ramp seemed to stretch on to infinity. My feet found uncertain holds on the ridged surface, slipped, gripped again. Deeklin passed by somewhere to my left, descending into his waiting audience, but my eyes stayed trained on the void of blackness that was the mouth of the ship. *Me personally.*

When I reached the top, I found myself in a room filled with bright blue light. The door closed behind me, and then I heard the buzz of the ramp retreating. No way out.

"Please prepare for cleansing," announced the same robotic voice from the microphone in its stilted Laffian language. "This is standard protocol. Please do not be alarmed." The light blinked a harsher blue, and then a light mist rained from the ceiling, dousing me in some kind of chemical that stung my skin. The outline of my body appeared on the wall in front of me, which I now realized was some kind of screen. Red dots appeared and enlarged, so that they became circles that moved over different parts of my body like your searchlights. The robotic voice announced something else, this time in what I now know is English: "No pathogens detected." The red circles disappeared, and then the blue light, leaving me in the blank box until what had been the screen wall swung back to become a door. The voice returned to Laffian. "Welcome to *The Santa Clara*, Tamalin."

"Long laffa," I said automatically.

Behind the door was a hallway, which, having no choice but to follow, I entered. My bare feet grew cold against the hard surface of the air-conditioned ship as I trekked down the passageway. Below the padding sound of my feet was the hum of an electrical song—a music I had not heard in a long time. I had the feeling of moving backward, of being a youth again, the entirety of space stretched before me. At the end of the hallway, I reached another door, this one marked with a foreign word and the symbol of a bird—an eagle, but of course you know that—and pressed my hand against the metal panel in the center.

Behind the door, the humans I had first spotted that morning waited for me.

From a distance, they had been beautiful. Up close, they were like trying to watch one of your old dome IMAX movies, with each panel showing its own piece of a complicated puzzle. My eyes went to the first face, its nose, the strange way it stretched like the slope of a steep hill, the anomaly of two nose holes, the little hairs barely visible from my view, the piece of something that had gotten stuck to one and now dangled in perpetual almost-falling.

Back out again: hair, holes, slope, nose, face.

The human attached to the nose said something. A light on a box attached to its chest blinked and then said in robotic Laffian, "Your friend Deeklin explained that he found our differences overwhelming. Don't worry, you will adjust. According to our ship's doctor, it might help your eyes to look past us rather than at us."

I blinked a few times and tried to look beyond, at the wall. Yes, they were correct; now I could see all five of them.

"Your people are lucky we heard your call," said one of the humans. This specimen had long brown hair held back by some kind of stretchy twine and two pins on either side of their forehead. "You saved them."

There was that word again. I frowned. "Where are you from?"

"A planet called Earth." A human with short hair and a square face touched a panel on their arm, which called up an image of a planet on the screen behind him. The planet was half Laffa, half Adalaffa—half land, half water—with swirls of white clouds like sefer milk in a mug of blueroot tea. I suddenly yearned for the sharp berry flavor labeled right from my mother's pot, and then thought of Fernin, our sefer, who had probably been chewing grass peacefully as the ashes rained down on her.

"Tamalin?"

The humans had been talking.

"What?"

"We said it is far away, in another galaxy far from yours," said the human, and then the box. "That is why it took us a year to go and return."

A galaxy far from yours. "This is not our galaxy," I clarified.

"Right. Deeklin explained your tragedy." The humans put their heads down. "We are sorry for your loss."

Something about their manner made me nervous. They had never met me; they had no investment in Laffa. Why the downcast faces and mournful expressions, as though it had been Earth, and not Laffa, that had perished? Or maybe it was their planet that made me nervous. All of that water.

Now that I know more about human deception, I realize I had the impression that we were all what you call "actors."

"My name is Captain Rosa," said the human with the long, pulled-back hair. "This," they waved to the square-faced human, "is First Mate Adin. We were both on the original *Santa Clara* expedition and heard your voice on the comms."

"Long laffa, Captain Rosa and First Mate Adin."

They also named Doctor Braun, an older human who reminded me of my father in a white lab coat and wrinkled pants. They did not introduce the others. Then they played a brief video about their species, including their distinct sexual attributes, and for some reason, this video made the crew blush. According to the film, Captain Rosa was likely a woman and First Mate Adin was likely a man, which was apparently an important distinction to make on Earth. I wondered if they were mates. The video also showed a few of your Earth cities, your typical food sources, and finally, the factories where so many of your products were mass-produced.

"Artisans like the Laffians are long extinct," said First Mate Adin. "Your people hold quite a special talent."

"It is no talent," I said. "We are just surviving."

"Of course." Captain Rosa elbowed First Mate Adin in what she must have thought was an imperceptible way. I wondered, for the first time, whether I was dealing with a less intelligent life form. "And again, we are very sorry for your—"

"Loss," I finished in English.

Captain Rosa and First Mate Adin exchanged a look. "How did you...?"

"You said that phrase before." I looked past them, at the cityscape of factories frozen on the screen. "I don't need a translator to learn, do I?"

Doctor Braun removed a computer from his pocket and stabbed frantically at the keyboard.

"So what is it you want with us?" I asked the humans, my eyes still trained on the stacks of smoke billowing from their roofs. "You're not just here to visit; I could ascertain that as soon as the other ships came into view. What could Adalaffa have that you want?"

Captain Rosa nodded to First Mate Adin. Behind them, an image taken from far above the planet appeared: an image of the water, and beneath it, as dense as spring grass, the seaweed that had both saved and cursed us.

"Seaweed?" I thought back to the image of Earth I had seen. "But surely you must have your own in all of that water of yours?"

Doctor Braun gave a strange choking sound—later, I would learn this was what you humans call sarcastic laughter. It was an unpleasant noise, and I winced.

"We do," said Captain Rosa, "though judging by our tests, your plants seem to be sentient. Ours are just…plants. Plus, all of those factories you saw have polluted our stock to the point that the negative aspects outweigh the positives."

"What positives?"

"Iodine, zinc, iron, vitamin K, B vitamins," Doctor Braun held out a hand and raised a finger for each item on the list, "not to mention the many antioxidants present." He lifted his other hand and waved those fingers too. "With all the pollution and cell damage on our planet, especially in Forager areas outside our protected cities, these vitamins have become even more important for our species' survival. Essential, even. We need your—"

"Our hope," Captain Rosa smiled, "is that we can trade with your people: service collecting seaweed for a one-way trip off this planet to another, more acceptable planet where the Laffians can thrive."

"You would give us a planet?"

The screen behind her shimmered and then revealed a planet that looked much like Laffa but with a few more lakes. "This planet is in the neighboring galaxy. Based on the research by Doctor Braun's team and their partners back on Earth, it is the closest to Laffa of any planet our ship has passed. And the best part? It's uninhabited."

The sphere in front of me turned and turned, and with every rotation, the green land hypnotized me further and further into a splendid stupor. I felt drunk. I felt elated.

Of course, you know what happened next.

####

I wonder, sometimes, about the humans on that vessel. I shuffle through their faces, the way a skilled card player shuffles their deck. What clues did I miss? What warnings? I focus, most often, on that one word used by Doctor Braun—pollution—and try to remember if I knew it, then.

You see, we have no word for pollution in laffian.

To pollute. To work, intentionally, against life. Had their computer translated "pollution" for me, it would have probably spit out a familiar term, a term that would have made me agree to anything but a one-way trip to Earth: *Adalaffa.*

But Doctor Braun hid another little fact, didn't he? A fact that I could not possibly have foreseen, but which, had he mentioned it, might have also translated, literally, to that same ominous word.

What had tipped your planet's environment so far off-balance that even your algae had become extinct? What had rendered your crops inedible, and brought your people to the point of starvation, and created such a stark contrast between city and countryside that those in the metropolises referred to their neighbors as Foragers?

$(O_2N_2CH_2)_3$, known by the name RDX.

Explosives.

And who, I might have wondered had I gotten to that obscured message, had been killing off your humans?

But of course, you know the answer, don't you?

I will tell you the rest, even though you know it.

"Thank you," I said. My hands went to my heart in the most genuine expression of Laffian gratitude. "Such a decision is not mine to make, but I will persuade the elders. With a new planet promised, they cannot possibly say no."

"Good." Captain Rosa put out her hand. I just stared at it, so she stepped forward to take mine. Her palm was very warm and dry. My fingers were much longer than hers, which made her grip seem like a child's. "Then it sounds like we have ourselves a—."

She used a word here that did not translate. However, when I look back at that first meeting, which of course the Captain had recorded without my knowledge in order to transfer the data to Earth, I now know very clearly what she said:

Deal.

What a human concept.

####

"Something does not feel right." Moramin sat on our mat with our new uniforms in her lap. An officer from *The Santa Clara* had been by to deliver them, sealed in something the humans called "plastic," just a few minutes before. The uniforms were a bleak gray, though one of a lighter shade and one darker.

"Don't be silly." I took my package and ripped open the smooth surface, which felt much like biting into the skin of a fruit. The fabric of the uniforms was thin and smooth—I would later learn this material was cotton—and sewn into a strange shape. "What are these long things attached to the shirt?"

Moramin extended the arms and held them up. Then she shrugged. No Laffian had ever seen a sleeve, let alone worn such a constricting garment. "As I said, something does not feel right."

There were other surprises: strange decorations of hard plastic that looked like they belonged on a necklace; odd holes in the top of the pants that ended in small sacks; little rows of teeth that came together and opened in an area one would usually consider private.

Buttons.

Pockets.

Zippers.

Moramin refused to try on her uniform, but I was eager to experiment. I discarded my tunic, long worn into a sun-bleached algae color, and slipped into the full cover of the uniform. The sleeves were too short and very uncomfortable, so I rolled the fabric almost to my elbows. Otherwise, I liked the feeling of the uniform.

I felt…human.

"You look ridiculous." Moramin could not help laughing, so she hid her smile behind her hand. "Like a sefer who's gotten stuck in a blue-root bush."

"I was just thinking of sefers earlier." I strutted around the room. "Remember blueroot tea?"

"Do I remember blueroot tea?" Moramin laughed again. "It was everyone's favorite drink."

"Not everyone. My father hated blueroot."

"Well, most people." She tossed the uniform on her lap aside and inched closer to me. "My father used to make blueroot biscuits. They were like rocks, but when you dunked them in the tea, they turned to sweet mush. Those biscuits fed us even during the hardest times."

Moramin had not grown up as I had. Her father had died young, an uncommon occurrence on Laffa, and her mother was a forest forager. She never mated again, which meant she and Moramin had no help and no other children to help them gather fungi. Moramin attributed her mechanical and weaving talents to many nights reaching into the small crevices beneath roots for the rarest mushrooms, though the patience required for such work was likely the most important earning from those difficult times.

"My mother used to say that to be Laffian was to be laffa itself," Moramin said. Her voice was suddenly serious, and her eyes looked some-where past me. "I'm telling you, Tamalin, those ships floating on our waters do not bring laffa with them. If you're not careful, they will snag you like seaweed and drag you down to their depths."

Typical Moramin, I thought as I left the hut to show the children, who were playing outside in the seaweed piles again, my new uniform. So skeptical, and yet so shortsighted. What choice did we have? If we refused the humans' offer, we would never get off Adalaffa; in a few generations, our people would all be green sea creatures swimming between the strands of seaweed like laffafish. The ways of our planet—our true planet—would disappear.

"What are those?" Sig asked, fingering the plastic decorations down the front of my shirt.

"I think they show rank," I explained, thinking of the military decorations I had seen on the uniforms of the officers.

Sig seemed impressed. He counted the five buttons down my chest. "You must be important, Papa."

"Of course I'm important, Sig." I pushed my chest out so that the buttons strained. "Wasn't it me who called the humans in the first place?"

####

That night, I dreamed of land.

I stood on it. Its solidness pushed back against the weight of my feet. Slowly, I stepped forward, and my feet left prints in the dust. I quickened my pace and then looked back; the prints were still there. When I jumped and landed, the impact of solid ground reverberated up my legs all the way to my hip joints.

The pain was excruciating and wonderful.

"My name is Tamalin," I whispered. My toes staked their small claims on the dirt. My soles bore down, rooting. "I am coming."

My name is Tamalin.

Even my dreams were warnings, and I still could not hear them.

####
####

The following day, we woke to a different landscape. The boats the humans had brought us had been unstacked, divided, and tethered to the five work ships in large webs. *The Santa Clara* was at the head of the whole operation, so that we would all move through the command ship and out into the new communities we would call home until our departure. In many ways, this was a smart strategy, for the seaweed under our own communities had been well reaped over the years to accommodate our own needs.

"Do you need help with your bag?" I asked Sig, who struggled under the weight of his sack. In it were his tunics and mat, which Moramin had packed for him that morning.

"I can do it, Papa," he said, shifting the strap on his shoulder. "I can't wait to see what is inside that ship."

Captain Rosa stood in the same spot as the day before, only this time, she was accompanied by a different set of officers. "Starting with those assigned dark gray uniforms, please approach *The Santa Clara* one family at a time," she commanded—or, rather, she spoke these words into her translator, which projected them across the water in a stately tone. "Those with all light gray uniforms, please wait until the dark gray uniforms have been assigned before coming aboard."

One by one, every member of my family and the four other families—Deeklin's, as well as three families of the elders who had been the first to speak in the human's favor—entered the same decontamination chamber and long hallway of my previous visit. We ended at the same gathering room, where a new video was paused on the image of a friendly face smiling into the camera. Based on my knowledge from the day before, this was a female human, and of the same coloring and general age as Captain Rosa.

"Welcome," said the friendly face as soon as we were all packed into the room. The mouth formed different words, but they had been translated into Laffian. "To those of you with dark gray uniforms, congratulations on your selection as the important factory overseers."

Please note that I say "overseers" here because that was the word your translator tried to form, and I want this testimony to be as accurate as possible. However, the word it actually used was "elders," which, as you know, had a very different meaning in Laffian. Even I, who had my sights set on elder selection one day, objected immediately.

"What's going on?" First Mate Adin had come in behind us and frozen the video. "Why all the chatter?"

"I am not an elder," I said.

"Me neither," said Deeklin. "I think you got the wrong Laffians."

First Mate Adin addressed his computer and then thought for a minute. Then he typed something, and the video rewound and then started again. "Welcome. To those of you with dark gray uniforms, congratulations on your selection as the important factory *leaders*."

Leaders still made me uneasy—our word for leader was often used as a synonym for elder—but it was not technically incorrect. The video played on, explaining that we five were each to be assigned a work ship where we would oversee the progress of our team's seaweed collection.

"I don't like this," Moramin hissed in my ear. "The elders should select—" She shut her mouth abruptly when the image of our new planet filled the screen. I looked from her wide eyes to those of my children, where the beauty of our potential home reflected in their green pupils. With any luck, their future children would never even know about seaweed or the life we had all lived on Adalaffa—though I selfishly hoped they would know my role in their survival.

According to the rest of the video, the work ships did everything except collect the seaweed, which is why the humans needed us. As Laffians dumped strands into a luge, the seaweed would travel into the belly of a great machine that would dry, crush, and mix the liquid. Plastic capsules collected this liquid into easily congestible amounts, and these capsules were carried on a conveyor belt, boxed, and sealed. Back on Earth, these capsules would save the 20 billion people sick from vitamin deficiencies.

We were their heroes.

As each ship met its quota of capsules, we would be packed on board and flown to our new planet. There, we would be dropped off—with supplies, of course—before the ship continued its course to Earth. Eventually, all the ships would earn their passage and leave Adalaffa's miserable salinity forever.

"Can't we wait for the other ships?" Moramin asked. "The people of Laffa should stay together."

"Unfortunately not," said First Mate Adin. "We humans have found that a little healthy competition makes for much faster work."

Again, you should note, here, that the word for "competition" did not translate. From the context, we understood that the rate of the work was an important factor to our new allies, and that they thought that pitting each ship against the others would make that factor increase; we did not understand the concept of gain for the individual through superiority over the group.

"Something does not feel right," Moramin repeated.

We exited the conference room through a door on our right. I wondered what was behind the third door—the one that led to the human quarters—and if, with enough persuasion, I might ever convince the captain to let me venture there. The right door took us to another hallway, which led us to a metal bridge that connected *The Santa Clara* to each of the five work ships by suspended metal walkways.

At the crossroads, we were divided.

"One family per ship," the crewmember in front of us commanded. He did not seem to care which of us went where. Sig broke into a sprint down the far left bridge, so we followed him, with the twins running to catch up and Moramin and I struggling with our bags.

"Look." Moramin pointed down. From this angle, with the ships blocking the suns' rays, we could see much further into the depths of seaweed below the water, which undulated with the waves and darting motions of laffafish.

"No, not the seaweed," she whispered, as if she could read my mind. "Lower."

My eyes strained.

There. A dark line, a crevice, visible only in fragments between the strands.

A subduction zone.

The bridge drifted slightly, its angle changed by the space between *The Santa Clara* and our work ship, and the line disappeared.

"Do you think it's active?" I asked.

"Not just active." She shivered. "About to slip."

"And the humans…?"

We looked at each other. Of course they knew. Their technology was far more advanced than ours; they had probably predicted our future earthquakes and tsunamis mere hours after scanning our planet.

The only reason they were allowing us to leave was that they had no choice but to save us.

"None of this matters," I said, turning away from the water. "I don't care about their motives. I hate this seaweed; in fact, I'd rip it all up myself if I could." My arms flexed in fury. "As long as they fly us off this cursed planet before the waves come, they can have every strand."

"I agree." Moramin lowered her voice even further. "But what makes you so sure they'll take us?"

The children called for us then, so I don't know what answer I would have given her.

Maybe I already knew there was no answer to give.

ARTICLE TEN

Excerpts of *From Diamonds to Dust:*

The Biography of HealthCorp's Justin Belore

Publication Date: April 1, 2120

Before the day of his birth, Justin Belore was already considered a miracle. His mother, Junie Belore, had been told from a young age that she would never produce a biological heir, and yet his father, Richard Belore, after looking at his wife one morning over his eggs Benedict as she suffered through a glass of cold ginger ale to combat a particularly horrible bout of "food poisoning," pronounced that he was going to have a son. No one believed him, not even Junie—that is, until she saw the darling jellybean on their private doctor's ultrasound machine.

Richard Belore was used to getting what he wanted. His parents, the Belores of Belore Diamonds, were worth over five billion dollars by the time they passed their company on to Richard. Only ten years later, Richard Belore was worth fifteen billion and rising. He had a knack for business, turned to craft by his years at Harvard Business School, and the reckless spending of the second generation of wealth.

Junie Belore, née Junie-Lee Jones, was cut from quite a different cloth—to be more specific, a plaid picnic blanket with grass stains on the bottom. Richard dug her up from the ground of the South, cleaned her up with a set of new dresses, and placed her delicately in a shiny New York City penthouse. All the eligible bachelorettes wondered what it was about this scrawny, pale-headed eighteen-year-old that had won Richard Belore's heart, but those who knew her well said that it was she—kind, altruistic, and completely shielded from the world—who was too good for Richard.

Whatever the case, they raised little Justin Belore with the rare combination of a love of wealth and a desire to do good in the world.

There were other influential events that nudged Justin Belore down the path that would end at HealthCorp. Both of his parents died at young ages from what are now—thanks to HealthCorp's funding—curable diseases. He then dated well-known animal rights activist Lance Martin for several years, during which time their frequent debates about the effectiveness of Lance's protests and a final messy breakup led Justin to spend $100,000 just to prove that he could save more animals with a new organic dog product company that donated 1% of their profits to rescue shelters than Lance had saved at every sign-waving spectacle in his whole career.

Justin won, of course.

Justin always won.

That dog product company did so well that Justin expanded Puppy Pure into Pets Pure and then People Pure, rebranded a few years later as HealthCorp. As the demand for diamonds decreased (this was during the height of the Wear Rubies campaign, founded by—you guessed it—Lance Martin), Justin transferred more and more of his energy into what he saw as the company of the future. By the time Belore Diamonds went bankrupt, Justin had completely moved his assets into HealthCorp, with the shiny new slogan "Our investment is you."

The final influence on Justin's career was another boyfriend, Frankie Nadir, known in their shared hometown of New York City as the Last Space Cowboy. Frankie was also the son of billionaires, but unlike Justin, Frankie had shirked his responsibilities as heir and looked to the stars as his path. He got a bachelor's degree in mathematics, a master's degree in computer science, several years of experience as a jet pilot, and a clean bill of health; he also got an invitation to a gala at Belore Mansion, where he met Justin Belore in person and the two fell in love. The records show that after that point Frankie's Russian tutor and personal trainer were paid for by Justin Belore, and then, soon after, that Frankie's lease expired and was not renewed.

Frankie had a profound effect on Justin. His love of the stars was infectious, and Belore Mansion soon upgraded its guesthouse into a private planetarium. From there, Justin charted Frankie's first journey into space, his second, and his last. In between these trips, Justin used Frankie's unique nutritional needs as inspiration for his Space Cowboy line, which included high-iron daily vitamins and green smoothies and which paid Frankie Nadir a high sum for his continued endorsements.

The two men were happy.

In fact, sources describe them as "soulmates." One friend who has asked to remain anonymous told me that she once walked in on Justin and Frankie slow dancing in the planetarium, the spiral arms of the Milky Way swirling around them in an endless Cosmic Year.

Happy, happy, happy.

And then Frankie Nadir was diagnosed with cancer.

####

The Milky Way is called a cannibalistic galaxy for its history of swallowing smaller galaxies.

During Frankie's illness, HealthCorp became that cannibalistic galaxy. One by one, smaller health companies were consumed, their technology melded with HealthCorp's to try to find a cure for Frankie's incurable disease.

"The doctors are wrong," Justin pronounced at the time, making headlines. "Nothing is incurable."

The search continued. Nothing on Earth seemed to help, so Justin expanded HealthCorp's holdings again, this time looking to the stars for answers he might have missed on Earth. He bought government secrets, hired engineers from all over the world, and founded a youth program for the geniuses of the next generation. The first spacecraft to enter interstellar space belonged to HealthCorp, as did the second, and the third, and the fourth. Then a fleet.

One of those voyagers, Marina Gee, who readers will also know as the inventor of the most successful living robot to date, was the one to discover the curative properties of hofellium. Perhaps this seems like an easy feat in and of itself, but keep in mind that HealthCorp's rovers had collected samples from over 500,000 planets. Hofellium, when swallowed in flakes like the rich swallowed gold, changed the physiological state of the consumer enough to kill most kinds of cancer cells. The flakes created their own negative effects, similar but at a higher intensity than the high levels of toxins causing problems for the whole human population at the time, but soon afterward, the seaweed from Adalaffa brought HealthCorp's next greatest product.

Frankie's cancer was cured, and HealthCorp was richer than ever.

But that's not the end of Justin Belore's legacy, is it?

Those of us alive during the guerrilla warfare of the early 2110s remember HealthCorp as a very different kind of influence.

Those of us who survived.

ARTICLE ELEVEN

Lia's Story

Curator's Note: "Lia's Story" was a 60-minute special originally aired on May 1, 2126. The special used the description of Lia's well-known account of Arrival Day and put her words over still images of her town, which was destroyed. "Lia's Story" has since been viewed as a controversial piece due to the obvious disconnect between the images and the actual words with which she describes the event—thus, I have chosen to include the transcript alone and not the accompanying film or photographs.

After the last bomb went off, everything was quiet. I could hear my heart like the bell that once rang in the center of town. I closed my eyes and tried to take a shallow, noiseless breath. My mom was crouched behind another beam with my little sister smothered in her grimy flannel shirt and my brother hidden in the crook of her arm. She reached around him to press a finger to her lips, and I nodded. We were all dusty from the debris, and my brother had a cut in his leg that had grown a large red patch on his thigh.

"All clear, Sir," a voice said from outside our door. "I think all known rebels have been eliminated."

My mom and I made eye contact. She shook her head no.

"Good. Kill a few more civilians to make the point, and then let's get out of here."

Two shots. A man screamed. Glass broke. A third shot. Then silence, although I did not trust my own ears.

I made eye contact with my mom again. She nodded so I stood up, my legs pained from crouching in the same position for over an hour. Then I tucked my hands into my pockets, feeling the familiar hole in the fabric, in order to calm their shaking.

"They're gone," she whispered. "Let's go."

My mom handed me the baby and took my brother up in her arms. "It's okay," I said to Adelaide, who stared up at me with her wide brown eyes and extended a chubby hand. We tiptoed out the back door and over the misshapen corpses of what had once been my mother's flowerbeds. The ground was loose and wet.

"Careful," warned Mom. We had no shoes, and there were nails and wood fragments littered over the whole yard.

We circled the house and stopped at the road. The front of the house was a pile of wood rubble, shingles, and siding. My grandfather had built the house with his own hands back when my mom's family had moved out of the city—out from under the thumb of HealthCorp—and my mom had refused to leave it ever since, even when my dad got a job offer from two of HealthCorp's top branches, ArmCo and then MediaCorp. *Don't you want to stop living paycheck to paycheck?* he had asked her one night, neither of them noticing I was listening from the hallway. *Not if the checks are signed by Anna Belore*, my mom retorted, followed by a string of curse words that I still can't repeat.

Maybe if they had left, my dad would still be alive. All that brain-power had to go toward something, and since it couldn't be Anna Belore's machines, it became weapons for the rebels. We had been lucky, Mom said, that he had been captured at a coworker's house and not ours, since the army had proven more than willing to kill kids that got in the way of their bullets.

Then again, I thought as I nudged a beam out of my path with my foot, maybe it was better to have a dead dad than a dad who indirectly helped blow up poor people's houses with their babies asleep inside.

"You all okay?" asked our neighbor, Mrs. Trelly, from what was left of her porch. She was still wearing her yellow nightie, and I could see the outline of her white underwear and saggy breasts under the thin cloth.

"Alive," said my mom. "You?"

Mrs. Trelly shrugged, as if to say, *Who even knows anymore?*

We walked the block between our house and the center of town and surveyed the damage. All the glass in the liquor store was blown out; same with the grocery. The sidewalk looked like the lake when the ice starts to melt—pretty but dangerous. A path of someone's blood trailed a few feet and then disappeared. Down the road in the distance, City Hall was completely flattened.

For a while we didn't see any bodies, but then we crossed the street and looked to the right, where the pediatrician's office backed onto the only office building, and found ourselves at an outdoor morgue. Ten dead men and women, two of which I recognized as people who hung around town handing out pamphlets and talking about HealthCorp's corruption like that was news to us. Apparently, they must have been doing more, and I wondered which of the other bodies were accomplices and which were people caught in the crossfire, like us.

I had seen pictures of people shot by HealthCorp bullets on the pamphlets, but up close, the wounds were much worse. You see, Health-Corp bullets didn't just go *through* people—they burrowed deep in the human tissue and left a toxin that slowly poisoned anyone not already dead from the shot. Thus, the ten people lying in front of me all had veins the color of rust—the color of hofellium—that had burst in certain places like squeezed tomatoes and spilled orange liquid onto the sidewalk.

"Wow," Bing said. He was four. He did not understand.

"Don't look," my mom told Bing as she covered his eyes—too late.

The baby began to cry, so I bounced her a little in my arms and turned her to look in the opposite direction.

"Maybe we should take Adelaide home," suggested Bing, not remembering that we didn't have a home anymore.

"We need to check on your uncle," my mom said. "Let's go."

####

Uncle Barney lived outside of town. I half expected his shack to be a pancake on the ground—especially since it had looked one strong wind gust away from blowing over even before HealthCorp's bombs went off—but even the strands of what had once been an American flag still flapped stubbornly from their pole.

"Uncle Barney?" I called out, remembering, too late, that I was holding Adelaide. She startled and then began crying. To calm her, I hummed "Twinkle Twinkle Little Star" and bounced her again.

"Lia?" He came out in an undershirt with brown stains at the pits and loose boxers. His eyes blinked in the sudden sunlight and then focused on us. "Oh, it's the whole family. To what do I owe the pleasure?"

Mom didn't seem to know what to say to that.

"We wanted to check on you," I said. "Didn't you hear the bombs?"

"Bombs?" Uncle Barney rubbed his eyes with his fists. Since I had last seen him at Dad's funeral, he had grown a beard and lost a patch of hair on the top of his head. "I guess I fell asleep with my headphones on again."

Mom clicked her tongue in her usual silent but disapproving way. Uncle Barney had trained to be an astronomer, but then he had "cracked up," as Dad put it, and been sent home from Yale with an offer to return when he got better. He never did. Given the chance, he would ramble on and on about creatures from other planets who were going to come to Earth and kill all of us. Three times, the sheriff had woken Dad in the middle of the night to get a naked Uncle Barney from the nearby fields where he had tried to burn crop circles into the corn. *Crop circles are supposed to come from the aliens, not us*, my dad had yelled at Uncle Barney over the phone a few times, as though the volume of his voice made any difference.

Now, we went inside the shack and stood inside the main room. The last time we kids had been allowed inside, Adelaide hadn't even been born yet. Not much about the furniture had changed—there were more empty beer bottles on the table, more cigarette holes burnt into the sofa from times Uncle Barney had fallen asleep while smoking, and more candy wrappers—but the walls were completely different. Uncle Barney had hung his bedsheets up as enormous canvases, and onto them, he had pinned up various news articles with certain words highlighted or circled.

"What are these?" Mom asked.

"Communications," Uncle Barney said, "between those of us who *know*."

"Know what?" I asked.

"That there's more out there," Uncle Barney waved his hand wildly above his head, "than metal and seaweed."

"Like what?" I asked, and Mom shook her head.

"Like them." Uncle Barney pointed to a blurry photo taken from very high up, like an airplane or a drone. In the photo were several fuzzy forms that looked like people—except for the fact that they were green. "Who do you think made all of those little pills you keep taking?"

Mom put the hand not holding Bing up to her forehead and rubbed very slowly from one temple to the other.

####
####

Uncle Barney didn't have much food in the house, but Mom said we would have to make do. "The grocery will be closed for two days," she explained after she called Mrs. Trelly to check. "They're still distributing seaweed, so I'll get those later tonight. The liquor store won't be open for weeks, but it seems," she opened a lower cabinet stacked with twelve packs, "that Uncle Barney has that food group covered. Good thing, too—I can trade these bottles for food."

She found some old pancake mix in the lazy Susan that just required water and a pan without a handle to cook them on, two eggs just past their expiration date that still sunk to the bottom when we tested them in a bowl of water, and some individual overripe bananas. Mom said Uncle Barney probably bought his groceries from the gas station nearby when he went to buy beer and cigarettes. None of us said very much after that. Uncle Barney said he had some work to do and disappeared into his bedroom, where the sound of scissors and paper revealed what Uncle Barney's usage of the word "work" meant.

"How long do we have to stay here?" asked Bing.

"Just a day," said Mom. "Or two."

She told me to go in and tell Uncle Barney that Adelaide needed a nap. The baby yawned on cue and turned her face into my chest. "Where should I put her?" I asked, thinking of the splinters of wood that had once been her crib.

"On the bed," Mom said with a shrug.

At Uncle Barney's door I knocked tentatively, then harder. No answer. I tried the knob, which was unlocked, and found the room empty. There was a bed with no sheets and a desk stacked with newspapers, one of which was still open and missing a few articles. I took off my sweatshirt and lay Adelaide down on top, then used the sleeves of the sweatshirt to swaddle her into the fabric. Almost immediately, she fell asleep.

Taking the opportunity to investigate, I sat down at Uncle Barney's desk and held up the newspaper. It was like a mouth with a few teeth missing. Even whole, the MediaCorp newspapers rarely had anything relevant to Allegany County or life in general outside of the five major metropolises owned and operated by HealthCorp, and reading about their newest subway trains or their pollution initiatives or their fancy parties felt like reading about a place on the other side of the world. Sure enough, the remaining articles in this issue contained coverage of some Feed-the-Foragers event at the Belore mansion, an update on the daily allowable dose of hofellium flakes, and an ad for seaweed pills with that same family, the Johnsons, smiling and looking healthy. Sometimes I would look at their round faces on the back of our seaweed bottle and think, *One day that'll be me.*

On other days, I knew better.

A gentle breeze flapped the corner of the paper, and I realized that the window was open behind the curtain. I got up to look and found myself face-to-face with a naked Uncle Barney, who was waving some kind of homemade device near his mouth and repeating a strange word: "Holaffa."

"Uncle Barney," I hissed. "Come in before Mom sees you."

He couldn't hear me, so I climbed out the window too and tapped him on the shoulder. His skin was hot, like he had a fever. When he turned around, his eyes were rapturous and unseeing. The pupils dilated and constricted. Was this what happened when adults got drunk? I had only ever seen the men who hung around the liquor store, and they usually just sat there.

"Uncle Barney?" I asked.

"They're almost here," he said happily. "Tonight, we must ready the circle!"

Mom was the maddest I'd seen her in a long time. *I told you I was gonna trade that liquor,* she kept yelling. *I told you a million times.*

She made Uncle Barney sleep on the couch, and the four of us took the bed. She had ripped down the sheets earlier while Uncle Barney yelled obscenities at her, and then she washed them in the old machine, so at least we didn't have to sleep directly on the sweat stains imprinted on Uncle Barney's bed. We all snuggled in together, and before we went to sleep, Mom told us all of the stories she could remember out of our book of fairy tales from home, including my favorite, which was "Rumpelstiltskin," and Bing's favorite, "The Frog Prince." I wondered if we would ever see the gold embossing on the cover ever again. Dad had found the collection at the library book sale years ago, back when I was the only child and Mom talked to me while looking at me, instead of Adelaide or Bing.

I knew it wasn't her fault, though.

After the stories, Mom put Adelaide in an empty dresser drawer and turned the light off. She stretched out on her side of the bed, and Bing tucked into her arm, which left me a whole half of a queen mattress to myself. Back home, I only had a twin I shared with Bing.

Soon, Bing began to snore in long, deep inhalations, and Mom's breathing became slow and regular. The room was warm from our body heat but not sweltering—which was good, since apparently Uncle Barney did not have air conditioning—but the stagnant air smelled like sweat and dust. We hadn't been able to take a bath; Uncle Barney's tub was what Mom called *unacceptable*, which meant peppered with mold and leaking water at the faucet.

After a few extra minutes, I slipped out of the sheet and put one foot on the wood floor, testing for creaks, and then the other foot. Step by careful step I moved to the door, where I turned the knob as slowly in case it squeaked. No sound. I slipped out and closed the door behind me, then pressed my ear to the crack, but from what I could tell, no one had even moved.

"I've been waiting for you," Uncle Barney's voice said loudly behind me.

I jumped about a foot in the air, but luckily my first instinct was to clamp my jaw closed and squeeze my arms tight to my body. Mom called this our startle reflex, and it did remind me of Adelaide waving her arms in silent terror when Bing woke her from a nap. *Quiet, calm, prepared.* This was Mom's mantra, the one that had saved us during several raids. Her kids knew better than to scream.

When I stopped shaking, I pressed my shaking finger to my lips and said, "Shhh!"

"Right." Uncle Barney imitated me. "Shhh."

We left the house and went outside to the porch, where the air was cooler. I wished I had my sweatshirt, but Mom had said using it as a swaddle was a good idea, and I felt weird taking it back. Uncle Barney must have seen me shaking, because he took off his own flannel button-down and handed it to me. Sweat and nicotine. Still, it was a nice gesture.

"What now?"

Uncle Barney pointed in the direction of one of the nearby fields. Then he took up a bag that I had not noticed lying under his old rocking chair and walked toward the corn. I thought, again, about what Dad had said—*Crop circles are supposed to come from the aliens*—and then followed him.

"Here." Uncle Barney handed me an unmarked bottle from his bag. I unscrewed the top and sniffed—gasoline—and then replaced the cap again. "I'll show you where."

Where turned out to be the entire cornfield. According to Uncle Barney, this was the location he had transmitted in his radio message, and we needed to clear a good spot for the ship or else forfeit our chance at being the first humans to welcome the aliens.

"Are they nice aliens?" I asked Uncle Barney. I was pretty sure that aliens weren't real and that he was as crazy as Mom said, but I was still curious, the way I had to know the ending of every book we started or else I couldn't sleep.

"Nice?" He shrugged. "Are we nice?"

I thought for a minute, remembering the shootings earlier that day, and shook my head no.

"Exactly. They aren't angels or something. If we push their buttons, they're going to push back."

We entered the field. The corn slapped at my arms and legs, so I used my feet to first push down the stalks and then dribbled gasoline on them. The smell made me cough. Some of the gasoline got on my bare feet and legs, and I hoped Uncle Barney didn't go full psychopath and light the corn on fire with me still in it. Still, I pressed on, sweeping the bottle from left to right and back again in long arches.

"Head back to the edge!" Uncle Barney yelled through the corn, so I followed my path back to the beginning. My feet were drenched, and I suddenly remembered that I was going to have to explain the smell to Mom the next morning. "Don't worry about your mom," Uncle Barney said when I came out of the corn, as though he could read my mind. "The ship will be explanation enough."

He took out a blue lighter and loose cigarette from the bag, lit the end, and took a long inhalation.

"Here's your vengeance, little brother," Uncle Barney said, and I realized he must be talking about Dad. "Hope you're somewhere with a good view."

Then he flicked the cigarette into the cornfield.

The fiery field was an orange wraith that burned and burned. For the first time all day, I felt at peace.

####

"What were you two thinking?" Mom yelled. She had Bing in one arm and Adelaide in the other. "You could have killed us all!"

Uncle Barney seemed unfazed. He took out another cigarette and lit it. "Lia and I had work to do."

"Lia is a child!"

"I'm twelve," I pointed out. "And it was just a bit of corn."

"A bit of corn?" My mom shook her head like she could not believe what she was hearing. "There's a farmer who makes his living off of that corn."

She had a point, and I finally felt bad, just like she wanted me to. It was hard enough to get by outside the city, even when you did have crops to sell to HealthCorp. What if some poor farmer's kid starved that winter because of me?

Uncle Barney didn't feel bad at all.

"None of that will matter now," he said, his eyes aimed upward at the stars. "They're coming."

"That's it." Mom turned away from him and started walking while she uttered her final pronouncements. "Sleeping in the street would be better than this. I thought that maybe you could put your delusions away for a few hours for the sake of the children, but apparently—"

"Look," Uncle Barney said to me, the only one who could still hear him, and Mom's voice faded to background noise. He pointed his finger up. "We did it."

Directly above our heads, the stars had been replaced by the lights of a sky-sized spacecraft.

####

The ship was like a blanket pulled over our heads, covering the stars and the moon as well as the light that emitted from the metropolis. We ran, but the ship seemed to follow us—or it was just that large. One by one, we stopped and waited to be flattened into the charred ground.

The ship rotated and let in the light again. Its thrusters emitted streams of orange and white light. Then it settled on the ground like an enormous bug, the eye of its command deck directly facing us.

HealthCorp, the ship proclaimed in large letters.

What had we done?

"We need to get away from here," my mother whispered, but she did not move. My brother was glued to her side, and the baby's eyes were wide with wonder. I couldn't move either, not even to tell her I wanted to stay. My breathing was shallow, as though the thrusters had burned all of the oxygen out of the air, and my heart pounded.

A door emerged in the hull of the ship and arced downward to the ground.

The next part seemed to happen on fast forward. One minute the ramp was empty, and the next, strange creatures flowed down the path and onto the field to settle into some kind of wall-like battle formation. My eyes could not adjust, and I saw them in pieces—a blue arm, a furry ear, a breastplate. I closed my eyes and reopened them. A bare green chest, a furry claw, a familiar HealthCorp gun. I rubbed my eyes until they burned and tried to refocus.

"Which of you is Uncle Barney?" a green mouth asked.

Uncle Barney stepped forward and then sank to his knees. "Holaf-fa," he said with a grand, sweeping gesture of his arm.

"Holaffa," the green mouth replied. It seemed to smile, though there was a hint of mocking in the expression. Now I saw the mouth was attached to a buzzed head about two feet higher than mine, and the bare chest, and many inked markings I realized were tattoos. "Where are your leaders?"

"Leaders?" Uncle Barney asked. "No leaders here."

The green mouth flattened into a line. "Are you not part of the company HealthCorp?"

"HealthCorp?" Uncle Barney stood up with difficulty and found his balance. "That's like asking if fleas can compete in a dog show."

"A dog show?" The mouth pursed in irritation. "Please explain."

"Well, a dog show is like a competition," Uncle Barney said as he began to rifle through his bag. At the motion, the aliens cocked their weapons. Uncle Barney found a cigarette, and once he put it in his mouth, the aliens relaxed. He rifled again, lit the cigarette, and returned the bag to his back. "Basically, a bunch of our pets run around a ring performing circus tricks and getting judged for their subservience."

"What?" asked the green mouth. "You're not making any—"

"A flea, on the other hand," Uncle Barney took a long drag, "is a little, parasitic insect that hangs onto the dog for its survival, even though it hates the dog and would kill it if it could."

"And these fleas are soldiers of HealthCorp?" asked the green mouth.

I looked at Mom as if to say *Help*, and she pursed her lips and handed me Bing and Adelaide. Then she stepped forward, in front of Uncle Barney, and cleared her throat.

"My name is Marie," she said, "and my husband was killed by HealthCorp's parent company. A lot of people in our town have been. We are no friends of HealthCorp, and if you are here to cause trouble for them—"

"We are not here to cause trouble," said the green mouth. That smile again, so disconcerting.

"Well," Mom said, "then I guess I'm confused—"

"We are here to do to HealthCorp with heavy hearts what their explorers did so easily to us."

"And that is…?"

"To kill."

Mom nodded, as though she had been expecting all of this. "Then you've come to the right corn field." She turned to me and gave me a strange look, like an apology or maybe regret, and then turned back to the aliens. "I know exactly how to take HealthCorp down."

ARTICLE TWELVE

Official Order for the Continuation of the Special Council

September 1, 2135

Though we had hoped to have an answer as to the decision of the HoFeLaffian occupation of Earth, the Special Committee tasked with deciding this planet's fate has deemed their work impossible in the timeframe imposed upon them. We know this news will come as a disappointment to many, and we ask for your patience as we extend the Council's adjudications for an additional five-year period.

To those who have submitted official documents and reports, as well as those who have sent personal journals or other written files from their collections, we say thank you. To those who would like to contribute to the Special Council's deliberations, please send your files as attachments to Aide@HFLCouncil.gov.

ARTICLE THIRTEEN

Exhibit G: Mallora's Diary, May 2140

Dear Diary,

Keeping a diary is apparently something humans used to do, and now that I'm basically human, I'm going to try it. I even got Mom to buy me real paper and ink!

I guess I should introduce myself, huh?

My name is Mallora, and I'm one of the HoFe in the HoFeLaffian species. Not that we're anything alike—but we're all aliens, I guess. I was just a baby when we landed here, and my dad died during the power grab. I don't remember much from that time, except that the city was very dark, and that my mom says I kept trying to make friends with the street cats whenever I saw one. Silly, right?

We actually have a cat now, Mr. Aduna. He's an orange tabby, and he's fifteen years old, which is close to the end of his lifespan. Mom likes to drag him out when we have human guests over—I think to remind them about the differences between us. Probably doesn't matter—humans see fur, and claws, and pink tongues, and bam, we're basically pets. Not that they'd ever say that out loud, of course. Not now.

Here he is, rubbing against my hand as I try to write this. Poor Mr. Aduna. I wonder if he'd be able to talk if his brain was bigger?

Well, that's all I have time for now!

-Mallora

#####

Dear Diary,

Mom got sick last week and sent me to Sora, who lives across the hall, for one of her poultices. Sora is about a thousand years old, and she smells like burned herbs and boiled socks. You'd think a HoFe with a heightened sense of smell would realize her apartment is stinking up the hallway, but no, Sora just stands at her fancy human stove all day and night cooking up weird medicines from the old world. You'd also think the building owners would do something about it, but apparently Sora healed his grandmother's shingles or something, so now she's immune.

Back to my story, before I went over, I put cotton in my nostrils to block some of the smells. "You'll offend her," Mom said when she saw my nose, but luckily, she was too feverish to actually make me pull them out. Sora noticed too, when she opened the door, but she let me in anyway. She had a new bald patch on the back of her head, and she walked with the use of a cane fashioned from a HoFe spear. Her dress was an extra-large tunic that dragged behind her like a bridal train.

"Do you know what's causing the fever?" she asked me.

"Yeah, the doctor says it's worms." I made a face. "Were there worms on HoFe?"

"Of course," said Sora, "but they didn't bother us."

Sora let me come through the living room to the back closet, where she kept her vials. The place was a wreck. Vines growing down from hanging pots, dried herbs on the table, crumbs crushed into the carpet at my feet. *Mr. Aduna keeps his litter box cleaner than this*, I thought.

"Bit of a mess, isn't it?" Sora said. I laughed awkwardly, but she didn't seem embarrassed. "It's the chaos of creation."

She disappeared into the darkness of the pantry and reemerged with two vials, one red and one blue. "The red one three times a day for three days," she said, marking the numbers on the vial in sharpie at the same time, "and then the blue one twice a day for a week."

"Thanks." I handed her a hundred-dollar bill. "Mom says to keep the extra."

Sora walked me to the door, but when we got there, she didn't open it right away. "What's your name again?"

"Mallora."

She nodded thoughtfully. "Well, Mallora, be careful out there. This planet is unkind to outsiders, and there's a lot worse than a few belly worms just waiting for you to let your guard down."

I had no idea what she was talking about. "Thanks," I said, putting my paw on the doorknob when it looked like she wasn't going to open it for me. "I'll take that under consideration."

What a weirdo.

-Mallora

####

Dear Diary,

I guess humans used to write about their crushes a lot in these books, so I'm going to tell you about mine. His name is Jonathan Gezul, and he is in the grade above me at school. I should just print his picture from the yearbook, because no words I use can do justice to the tall, dark-haired, freckled human who says hello as he puts his backpack in the locker next to mine every morning.

Jonathan Gezul.

Of course, he has a girlfriend, Nora. She's human too, and she is mean, mean, mean. Last year, she had everyone calling me Cat Lady, which doesn't even make sense, since a Cat Lady is a human who owns a lot of cats.

Anyway, I hate her.

It's hard enough being one of only three HoFeLaffians in my school, with one being a Laffian and the other being the worst kind of HoFe—a traditionalist. He even wears a shield to school! And they let him, because it's technically illegal to discriminate against a HoFeLaffian, though even I wouldn't blame them for it. *A shield.* Can you imagine it? All shiny and clanging into his desk during the lessons.

Back to Nora. I think she must feel threatened by me, because she's always spreading rumors about the HoFe that seem aimed at me. For a year she had the school convinced I had fleas, and before that, she told all the boys that HoFe girls marked our mates by clawing their faces. Unfortunately, they were just dumb enough to believe it, and even though the principal has since set the record straight, I still get nervous stares and the occasional hand over a blushing cheek.

Sigh.

-Mallora

####

Dear Diary,

Well, Nora's done it again, and I literally can only stop crying long enough to write a few lines. She saw me talking to Jonathan this morning—the way we were both smiling and laughing, like we were the couple instead of them—and I guess she decided it was time to remind me who was queen of the jungle. When I left lunch, her squad cornered me, and…and…they shaved my head. Not just the top, but all the hair on my face, which now looks like moon with its wide, pale surface and deep craters. Plus, she got my whiskers, which means that I can barely stand up before getting so nauseous that I vomit. Sora made me a drink that really helps, but I can only drink it a few times a day—not long enough to attend school. Mom says she's going to talk to the principal this afternoon, and that, unless she feels sure he'll take firm action, she's going to pull me out and homeschool me like a lot of the other HoFeLaffians.

Basically, my life is over.

-Mallora

####

Dear Diary,

No more school. No more Jonathan. No more anything.

####

Curator's Note: This is the final entry in Mallora's diary; a week later, she fell from the roof of her apartment building. Her mother claimed it was an accident, dizzy as Mallora was from the lack of whiskers and a potential overdose of prescribed potion, but many witnesses say they believe the fall was an intentional jump. That year alone, fifteen HoFeLaffian teens committed suicide—fifteen more than had ever done so in the whole history of all three planets. Her diary was used by police during their investigation and then passed to the Society for the Wellness of HoFeLaffian Teens.

ARTICLE FOURTEEN

Recording of the Three Tams

Location: *The Santa Clara*

The work ship was a monstrous beast. Into its fiery mouth we threw handfuls of seaweed, and we watched in awe as it gnashed, gnashed, gnashed its teeth against the thick fibers of its salty eats. Flecks pasted our faces in green, though you could not tell until later, when we peeled the dried seaweed off like another layer of skin.

We were the fastest gatherers. Our crew called us the Three Tams, and as we shoveled in our finds, they muttered *Tam! Tam! Tam!* Tamalin's first three children; Tamalin's most important assets.

They were not jealous, for the more we fed the beast, the higher the number on the screen above the conveyer belt shuffled forward, one load closer to 1,000,000.

At 1,000,000, we would go home.

Yet in truth, we moved slower than we could have, for Adalaffa was our home. Unlike the elders who yearned for Laffa, we loved the feeling of salt whipping our faces on a windy day. The suns were familiar faces waking us each morning. The seaweed wholly sustained us. At night, we drank cups of gin and admired the stars. Adalaffa felt like it had been made for us, though we knew the truth was the other way around.

And yes, we could admit Adalaffa had its faults too. The great tsunami that had sent a wave over the entire planet, for example, that we had watched destroy the basket villages that had once been our homes from the ships held in pause at a safe distance above the water.

"Why aren't we moving?" Papa had asked Captain Rosa. As family of factory leaders, we had been permitted on *The Santa Clara* for the journey, and our viewpoint was the command deck of that great human hub.

"Our orders have changed," said Captain Rosa, refusing to look him in the eye. "We are to wait and watch. If the water dies down and the seismic activity stops, we are to return to Adalaffa until we meet our new quota."

"But we were promised—"

"What choice do you have? You need us to carry you away before Adalaffa destroys itself, and we need you to meet your quotas before we'll move you anywhere." Captain Rosa finally looked at him, her face devoid of its usual softness. "You're stuck, Tamalin. HealthCorp owns all of us now."

If our mother had been there, she would have spoken up. Maybe she would have even hit Captain Rosa across her defeated face. When working conditions had gotten bad, and she had lost the baby, and we had not a single day of the week to rest or replenish our own feed supplies, it had been Moramin who had led the strike—a strike against the figurehead of her own spouse—until the humans had shown us the guns that harnessed their true power.

We could still picture her there, at the door of the work ship, with her legs wide and her arms outstretched to stop us from entering.

We could still picture her alive.

"At 1,000,000 you'll take us?" Papa had asked Captain Rosa. He had put out his hand in the human gesture of friendship.

"I promise," Captain Rosa had said.

####

Are you already uncomfortable?

Do you have that feeling deep in your stomach, that feeling that the world you thought you knew so well has suddenly disappeared?

Welcome to Adalaffa.

####

264,399.

264,400.

264,401.

Tam! Tam! Tam!

####

Another tsunami. This one came without warning, and we barely made it to the work ships in time to levitate above the water. The boats the humans brought us went under like your surfers, and the wave took them for good.

Our homes were gone.

The few belongings we had saved from the *LaffaLaffa* were gone.

The gin was gone.

When the work ships landed, our father and the other elders had to teach the younger children how to weave.

Like reeds, our people were winding round and round our spokes.

####

421,765.

421,766.

421,767.

Tam! Tam! Tam!

####

We took on the stylistic distinctions of our captors.

Bren cut their hair short, almost to the scalp. They were the largest of us, a mountain, which was a word we only know from our elders. It
was hard to imagine, this idea of mountain, this mass blocking the endless
sky, this steep terrain, just as Bren was hard to take in with a glance. They
scowled a lot. They hunched their shoulders.

Ven was like a seaweed strand. They grew their hair long and in
braids, like our mother's. They pierced one ear and the opposite eyebrow.
They carried two knives attached to their belt, which at any moment they
might whip upward in a spinning display of skill and threat. Not toward
the humans, of course. Not toward us. Their arms were the terrain of lean
muscle, and their waist was a wall.

Sig became a cartographer, and their body the map. Tattoos covered
both arms, both legs, the chest. The head, which was shaved. These tattoos
cost gin, but Sig would gladly pay the gig artist on *The Santa Clara* their
share for another mark. Sig often went shirtless, adorned only with strands
of white beads cut from the bones of laffafish and strung on dried seaweed
hemp they wove themselves. The story of Adalaffa played out across their

skin, as though we needed a reminder of our basket lives, our fishermen hours, our captivity.

These are not stories for us, Sig said.

Many Adalaffians began mating earlier. What else have our people to do in our free time but drink and reproduce? None of the Tams paired, however; there was something that made us hesitate, something about the way our mother used to hiss and warn and was ignored that hinted at mating as a kind of servitude.

The Three Tams had enough of bondage.

We wanted freedom.

At night, when only the three of us remained in our hut, we whispered about our desires. To force the humans off Adalaffa. To return to the simple ways of the sea.

Perhaps we could build tall bridges, Ven suggested, so that when the tsunamis come, we will not be washed away?

Perhaps we could steal one of the humans' ships? Bren mused. One could hold all of us for a short time.

But there were obstacles. We listed them: Their numbers are greater. Their technology is incomprehensible. They have more advanced weapons. The tsunamis could return.

Let's just kill them all and get it over with, Sig said.

But how?

What did you say?

You don't like the way we are telling our story?

Too bad.

601,244.

601,245.

601,246.

Tam! Tam! Tam!

Our father did not just take on the human design; he became one of them, from his leather shoes to his standard-issue uniform to his dyed blond hair. The only Adalaffian traits remaining were his blue skin, which he powdered a dusty tan, and his size, which was too tall to be human, even when he hunched. He rarely came to the work ship anymore, preferring to drink on *The Santa Clara* with his human compatriots.

Besides, he trusted his Tams to keep production in check.

And what did the humans gain from his company?

Eyes.

Ears.

Hints when an Adalaffian began the inevitable transformation from complaint to action.

Our mother would have done something about his betrayal, but we were not our mother. We worked our bodies like animals; our mouths stayed closed tight. When Tamalin did visit the work ship, we hauled seaweed into the insatiable mouth as fast as we could and waited for praise. When Tamalin did not visit the work ship, we hushed our haulers anyway, for fear that he might appear behind them with a flask in his hand and a sarcastic smile on his lips.

Tamalin.

Caller of humans.

Savior of our people.

These were the stories he told our work ship, and the others who now served under him, his first mates. Yet our father had no place on Sig's mural, and no place in the hearts of the people who cursed his name as they hauled and hauled and hauled the bounties of our endless sea.

####

723,456.

723,457.

723,458.

Tam! Tam! Tam!

####

We had one day off a week, which the humans called a "sacred" day and which meant we had a full twenty-four hours off. Suns Day. On Suns Day, we began a new tradition of communing with our neighbors. Adalaffa bread, seaweed jam, and gin were the staples, with the occasional rare item from the humans—a red sugar packet that solidified in water and became a gelatinous delicacy; an arched noodle that, when mixed with a different orange packet, became a gooey main course; a web of noodles that, when mixed with a yellow packet, turned plain water into a soup. Everything from the humans was delivered with a shake, rip, and pour.

One Suns Day, it was our turn to host. The neighbors from the four nearby boats came with the Adalaffian staples carried in their only pots, and we supplied the rare dish, a dried seaweed stick dipped in a jar of brown mud distributed by Ven with a hand flourish and a bow.

"What is it?" they asked.

"Try it."

The dish was thick, crunchy, and a little sweet. "Peanut butter," we told them, and they repeated the unfamiliar words, "peanut butter," with awe. Unlike jam, the butter was hearty, and it gave us a full belly feeling we rarely achieved with seaweed. Ven distributed a second stick, and then a third, until all that was left was a coating in the jar he collected with breadcrumbs and shook into an empty pan for the children.

"The best human food yet," we agreed.

After the gin, Sig got out the shakers we had made with empty food cans and dried seaweed pieces and gave one to each of the children. "Let's start with 'Long Laffa,'" they said, which was smart since even the youngest child knew the simple refrain of our national song. Sig had the best voice, our mother's voice, and as they hummed the first note and shook their beads, the group could not help smiling at the promise of a treat rarer than even peanut butter. *Laffa,* Sig chanted, *long laffa,* and the little children repeated, their notes slightly off-key. *A gift, long laffa, a song, long laffa.* Some of the adults took up spoons and empty pots, while others clapped and slapped their legs. *We thank you, long laffa, and pass on long laffa.*

Sig's eyes were closed as they repeated the refrain. *Laffa, laffa, laffa, laffa.*

Many of us found ourselves crying, though we did not know exactly why. Long laffa, long life—and yet also a planet, the home that we had been taught to long for but would never know.

Later that night, after the guests had wandered home, the three of us sat facing the water.

"This planet is also laffa," said Bren, as though continuing a previous conversation. We were surprised—Bren rarely spoke, even when it was just the three of us.

"Everything is laffa," agreed Ven.

"So then why work so hard to leave?" Sig asked. "Our history is here." Their tapestry skin seemed a reminder, or a reprimand.

"Because we do not belong here," said Ven. "This planet is laffa, but we are not a part of it. Sooner or later, the water will cast us out."

The three of us looked at the sea.

####
####

Another tsunami.

More days away from the work ships building new boats.

We wove and wove until our hands were raw. We are almost there, the Adalaffians said to their neighbors as they shared their seaweed ointment. Soon we will have a new planet, and we will never eat another strand of seaweed again.

A week later, the humans announced that our first 750,000 pillboxes had been taken to Earth, and that we had a new goal: 2,000,000 pillboxes.

####

Let us guess.

You feel guilty, and yet at the same time detached from those star-travelling humans on *The Santa Clara*? You wonder what any of this has to do with you, the Earth walkers, the innocent?

We know all about how you feel. In fact, we learned the word from your translator.

Disassociated.

Go ahead. Take your seaweed pill.

We'll wait.

####

During the next month, seaweed collection decelerated. We did not dawdle our hands intentionally, nor calm the pace at which we hauled the seaweed up from the water, and yet, the numbers slowed.

We carried the weight of our doubt on our backs.

We grew tired.

"Think of the new planet," Tamalin told us on the loudspeaker; yet we were not strands of seaweed, so easily fooled into reaching for the same bait.

Our shoulders tensed, and our fists clenched.

One day, a Laffian in our crew named Brayadin collapsed while feeding seaweed into the mouth of the machine. We got her upright, but she seemed uneasy, like she was on a rocking boat. Her stumbling feet might have reminded you of rabbits leaping, crossing, leaping through underbrush. Her blue eyes did not seem to focus on any of our faces.

"Drink some water and keep moving," said one of the human guards who kept watch.

The guards wore different colored uniforms, but a majority of them were red with blue and white lettering, including the one talking to us about Brayadin. According to our father, these humans were from the space program of a place called the United States of America, which was one of many things called "countries" that claimed specific lands on Earth as their own. What a strange concept, we thought. Back home, the elders had represented all Laffians; on Adalaffa, we only had neighborhoods due to the physical constraint of forming a web of bridges in order to tether individual boats to the main ship.

All Laffians were part of Laffa, and Laffa was all.

Yet these humans seemed to take their uniform colors very seriously. They also seemed to know as little about each other as they did about us, so that, in the middle of conversations, they would often refer to their translators or the handheld machines that spit back data in response to their anxious fingers. This happened now, as another guard in a rare green uniform asked the guard in the red uniform what had occurred. Neither guard moved from their posts as they spoke, and both kept a hand on the unknown machines always at their belts.

"She needs medical attention," Sig insisted.

"She's fine," the red-uniformed guard replied. "Keep moving. We're already a few hundred pills behind today."

The guard was nervous, we realized. Something was at stake for her. For the first time, we wondered about these humans who had left everything behind to gather a bunch of seaweed on a water planet so far from home. What had they been paid—and what had they sacrificed?

Brayadin insisted that she was fine, and though we knew she was not, we all went back to work. We hauled, hauled, hauled seaweed out of the water and fed, fed, fed the machine.

The day dragged.

The suns moved across the sky.

That night, Ven, who had the best hearing of the three of us, woke to a strange cry from a nearby boat. "Sig. Bren. Get up." Sig shot up out of bed, an inked black tapestry naked from the waist up, as usual; Bren had to be shaken and then hauled up onto their feet. We threw on tunics and ran. The cry had lessened slightly, but for some reason, the strangled sound was more disturbing. Think of a red fox's call in the dark. A few other Laffians had awoken too, and they followed us to the boat, stumbling, as we did, over the bump where the bridge connected. No one was in the hut, but on the deck on the other side, we found a body prone on the ground and a child crouched over it, producing the terrible call.

The prone body was Brayadin's.

And Brayadin was dead.

"Laffa?" the child wailed.

No one replied.

Laffian custom requires a fifty-day funeral, during which the fifty laffas must be recited by an elder and echoed by the surviving family members every day over the body and then, after the burial on the seventh day, over the ground where the Laffian lies. We had made do on Adalaffa by sending the bodies of the dead into the water and saying the fifty laffas facing the sea, with the elders and the family members as the only witnesses to the tradition. However, for many reasons—since Brayadin had been a part of our crew, and since her only surviving child was just a toddler, and since her spouse had separated from her and recoupled, and since the elder in charge of her ceremony was a part of our crew, and really, if we are being honest, since we felt somewhat responsible—we decided to take it upon ourselves to complete the fifty laffas on the deck of the work ship every morning.

Our human guards did not understand.

"Can't you do the laffas after work hours?" they asked.

"The suns will be down," we said. "The fifty laffas must be during daylight."

"Why?"

"Because that is the way the funeral has always been done."

We could not understand why this answer did not satisfy them.

For three days, they let us complete the laffas; still, we could feel them watching from the second-floor deck, growing more and more anxious. On the fourth day, when a rare haze turned the suns green and we paused to watch after only twenty of the fifty laffas, one of the guards called down, "Hurry up and get back to work. Do you know how far behind quota we are?"

Quota.

Laffa.

Quota.

Laffa.

Looking back, we cannot agree as to exactly what happened in that moment. Sig calls it Justice. Bren calls it Revenge. Ven calls it an Accident, a strange convergence of emotions and circumstances. We know it was none of those things.

We do know that the Laffians ignored the human guards, and that the guards took from their holsters the black machines that had until that point been just accessories. We do know that these machines pointed at us, the mourning Laffians, and that they were accompanied by the words, "We said get back to work." We know the machines sent a strange fear through us, so that we froze there, on the deck, with the hazy green suns at our backs, unable to run.

We know the sound that came next; we can never forget it, even now that we are almost elders ourselves.

Boom. Boom.

We looked around us, but no Laffians had fallen. Instead, two thumps above and the empty space on the second story deck indicated that it had been the humans, not us, who had been hit. But how?

A third black machine, raised and glinting as the suns emerged from their haze, slowly came into view from the ship's shadow.

Behind it came our father.

####

There was not one word spoken between us to decide our plan.

The three of us had never had much use for words anyway.

We charged into the work ship like one of your wolf packs, with Bren leading as alpha. They barreled into the confused human closest to the door, who Ven cleverly caught and used as a shield against the shots fired by the other three guards on duty. Blood came from the body like water from a shaken strand of seaweed and splattered our tunics, our faces, our hair. Bren took a bullet in their left shoulder, but the hit did not stop them; they swung their right elbow into the face of the guard who had fired the shot and then knocked the man down with a chest thump. Ven's knives swung up into their hands and then became a blurred hurricane as they whipped their body to give the knives force. Their braids became one solid top spun and then abruptly stopped as the momentum moved to the flying knives, *shwup shwup*. The body of the third guard fell forward.

There was still one guard, the fourth, who normally kept watch from the second-floor walkway. He had raised the steps so that we could not get to him and found a hiding spot behind the control panel, from which vantage point we knew he would soon pick us off like a hunter picks birds off of a flock. The bullets banged off the metal structures, went through the ship's walls, came closer.

Too close.

"Back, back!" Ven commanded.

Ven and Bren retreated, but Sig, angry Sig, could never back down from a challenge. They ran forward and, using a control panel as a springboard, jumped up five feet in the air. Their hand found the lowest railing of the walkway and hauled up their hundred and fifty pounds with one arm, like an empty net from the sea. They deposited that weight onto the walkway with a roll across the metal mesh and then found shelter on the other side of the control panel the human used as a shield. Watching them move was like watching one of your ballet dancers pirouette across a stage. Such beauty. Such display of life. We were in awe.

"Laffa!" pleaded the guard in Laffian. "Please! Laffa!"

Sig closed their eyes and took a deep breath. "This is not Laffa," they said. "It's Adalaffa, and you're the ones who trapped us here." Then they pounced, their body rising several feet in the air over the control panel and human and landing on both feet on the other side. The human fired, but Sig had already knocked aside the gun, so that the shots went wildly into the metal siding. Sig's other arm grabbed the mouth of the gun, pointed it down, and twisted it away from the human. They paused there, machine ready to kill.

Sig took another breath.

"Tell us how to win, and I'll leave you with your laffa."

####

The weapons store was behind a fake wall, where the guards had been instructed to retreat to in case of an uprising. Ten guns, strapped in and loaded. In our large hands, they were small but heavy. The other crewmembers practiced raising them and aiming.

"Follow our lead," we said.

Tam! Tam! Tam!

Tam! Tam! Tam!

Tam! Tam! Tam!

####

The Santa Clara was a bloody sea.

Human bodies lay dead or dying in the hallways. Those who could fight aimed their weapons and were taken down. Their insides flowed out in a shade of red we had never seen. Their screams were worse than the wails of a mourning ceremony.

The Three Tams tuned these noises out like the waves of the ocean against a hull. We had taken the command deck, where three living humans—Captain Rosa, First Mate Adin, and the woman in the pilot seat—stood with their hands in the air. Behind them, screens flashed and several computerized voices proclaimed breaches all over the ship.

Our father entered the room. He had red blood on his leather shoes, and as he approached, he left red footprints in his wake.

"Reason with your children, Tamalin," Captain Rosa commanded.

"You should have learned more about our culture, Captain Rosa," our father said in the language of the humans as he approached her. How had he learned it? "Most specifically, the first rule of laffa: if you take someone else's laffa, you forfeit your own." He slipped behind her to take her seat, and his shoulders relaxed into the back of the command chair. He looked like he belonged there. "Now let's find out if all of my years of observations have…what is your expression, again? 'Borne fruit?'"

He hit a few buttons on the control panel on his armrest, and the ship's emergency systems stopped flashing and proclaiming. The command deck was silent, but for the heavy breathing of the humans—we realized now that we had been holding ours—and our father's quick typing. The screen changed again, charting a course for the planet we had seen just briefly during our orientation.

"And it seems I no longer need to observe you, Captain Rosa" Tamalin said in Laffian. "And as the first rule of laffa states—"

Tam! Tam! Tam!

ARTICLE FIFTEEN

"Welcome to Earth!" General Script

Curator's Note: I must admit that the inclusion of this script is an indulgence of mine—it is not, necessarily, of vital importance to the Special Council's decision. However, I had little in the way of evidence showing any positive accommodations the humans made upon our arrival, so my hope is that this piece, though wildly unsuccessful in practice, might live again as a symbol of the complexity of human nature—and the resilience of enterprise.

"My name is [name], and I will be your official Welcome to Earth© tour guide!"

> *Guide notes: HoFeLaffians refer to themselves by first name only, and we encourage you to do the same to avoid offense.*

"Before we get started, let me be the first to say welcome to your new home! We are so happy to have you. If you have not already adjusted your translator, please do so now."

> *Guide notes: To reset the translator, press the red button*

on the side and then the button that says "Listen." After
pressing these buttons, please speak into the translator to
allow the machine to identify your language of choice. You
may also select a language manually using the "Choose
Language" button and then scrolling with the blue arrows,
though this will take a great deal more time.

"My job, as Welcome to Earth© emissary for your chosen country, is to catch you up on history, music, foods, and slangs you might need to know using our advanced virtual tour technology. So sit back, relax, and take in the scenery of beautiful [country name]."

Guide notes: Here, the screen will show a sweep of your
country's landscape. Remember, some of the HoFe partic-
ipants in the group may experience motion sickness and
vomit a brown, chunky liquid during this time, so please
remind them of the bags tucked inside their brochures.
Under no circumstances should you offer a well-meaning
comparison to your cat's throw-up.

"First on our tour are the national landmarks. If you look to your right, you will see [capital name], the capital of [country name]. Here, the government, which used to be a [form of government] before HealthCorp's takeover and then your blessed arrival, ruled its people. To your left is a selection of national treasures, including [landmark], [landmark], and [landmark]."

Guide notes: Several of your listed landmarks may have

been destroyed on Arrival Day or during the resulting riots.
If you believe your tour needs to be updated, please contact
the Help Desk.

"Do you hear that? That's the sound of [music genre], this country's most well-known type of music. Throughout the rest of the tour, you will hear famous singers like [singer name] and [singer name] serenading your ears."

Guide notes: Tour guides do have some flexibility in this area, so feel free to suggest songs to your Team Lead. Playlists should span at least a hundred and fifty years and lean toward the historical to give our new citizens some cultural context. Please include the global phenomenon "Oh Hey, HoFeLaffians!" as your final song to give your participants a sense of belonging.

Here is a sample from the United States tour:

1. *"Dream a Little Dream of Me" – Ozzie Nelson – 1931*

2. *"I Don't Want to Set the World on Fire" – The Ink Spots – 1941*

3. *"All Shook Up" – Elvis Presley – 1957*

4. *"Come Together" – The Beatles – 1969*

5. *"Dancing Queen" –ABBA – 1976*

6. *"Billie Jean" – Michael Jackson – 1982*

7. *"Wannabe" – Spice Girls – 1996*

8. *"Crazy in Love" – Beyoncé – 2003*

9. *"Text You Later" – Baby Boys – 2028*

10. *"Quarantine Summer" – The Warmers – 2040*

11. *"The Bot-Bot Dance" – Wanda Wang – 2090*

12. *"Twenty-Second Century Love" – Billy Kanumba – 2100*

13. *"Oh Hey, HoFeLaffians!" – Light Speed – 2125*

Under no circumstances should you include songs in which aliens play a role or songs that feature the apocalypse, including, but not limited to, "It's the End of the World" by R.E.M., "The Purple People Eater" by Sheb Wooley, and "E.T." by Katy Perry featuring Kanye West.

"As you continue on your travels, please keep in mind that the people of this country:

a. Have submitted to HoFeLaffian rule. They are very welcoming and might even worship you.

b. Put up a fight upon your arrival but have since been controlled. Please be cautious when interacting with locals. Do not do any of the following:

   ☐ Accept food from strangers.

   ☐ Hold packages for people who claim they will "Be right back."

   ☐ Walk alone at night.

   ☐ [Other common attack methods prominent in your area]."

Guide notes: Please star, highlight, or otherwise mark which of the two letter options applies to your tour country. Please also feel free to add bullets of other potentially hazardous activities common in your region.

"Should you have an incident during which you feel discriminated against or even threatened, please contact your local HoFeLaffa rights group immediately at 1-800-PRO-HO-LA.

Guide notes: Encourage your participants to write this number down and keep it handy. As an extra precaution, Welcome to Earth© has included this number on the back of the brochure, on security bracelets in our participant gift bags, and on many sponsored billboards around all major cities.

"Now that you have a familiarity with the sights, sounds, and general demeanor of your new home country of [country name], I hope you feel right at home. Welcome, and long laffa!"

ARTICLE SIXTEEN

Tanner's Deposition

August 6, 2131

I really didn't want to come here today—didn't even want to think about any of this ever again—but a Council subpoena is not exactly the kind of document you can just receive from your hometown sheriff and then throw away. Honestly, since the attack on HealthCorp, I've basically been living in my mom's basement playing video games and avoiding all human contact.

Yeah, I guess you could say I'm not doing that well—but I'm alive, aren't I?

There are a lot of people—a lot of friends—who can't say the same.

Anna Belore was my boss. Not in the vague, *I knew her so well* way you see witnesses talk about on the news, but my real boss, the woman who sat at the big desk right on the other side of the glass. She hired me straight from Princeton, said she could only trust a fellow alumnus to be her new assistant, and I was honored, really, to get the chance to earn someone like Anna's trust. She was an idol of mine, a kickass CEO, and I thought checking her emails and scheduling her meetings could rub some of that powerful juju off onto me. Every morning when I dropped off her seaweed smoothie, I would take a deep breath of that purified office air and think, *This is going to be me someday.*

Sure, there were parts of Anna's work I didn't exactly approve of, but it wasn't my job to decide whether selling bullets to the army was "ethical" or "moral" or whatever. I was there to answer the phones with a chipper *Hello, Anna Belore's office, how may I direct your call?*, and I did that, with pleasure, for five years.

In that time, I made more money than most people make by the time they retire.

How many twenty-six-year-olds do you know who own an apartment on the Upper West Side?

I also learned a lot about Anna in that time. What she loved—seaweed smoothies, black leggings, a good old-fashioned bidding war—and what she hated. At the top of that list were any mention of her father, Justin Belore, and the smell of cheap perfume. In fact, they had the same effect: after a visiting client came through wearing knock-off Chanel or waving her father's name around like knowing him would secure their contract,

Anna had me move her to her secret office on the floor below while I sprayed a $1,000 bottle of HealthCorp's *Eau d'Anna* around the room. Imagine orange blossoms and roses, with an undertone of incense.

I always snuck a few sprays onto my wrists—as I quickly learned, girls go crazy for a man who smells like summer.

Why did she hate her father? I'm not really sure. I remember one time after a client left, I found Anna spraying *Eau d'Anna* directly onto her neck in angry pumps and mumbling to herself, "National hero? Please. He wasted his inheritance searching the stars for the sorcerer's stone. I'm the one who built the empire." By the time she noticed me, her shirt collar was drenched and her face was as red as she got after a hard workout at the HealthCorp gym.

As time went on, her distaste for Justin Belore's memory increased. It made her paranoid. She thought every Board member was thinking of him when they objected to a new initiative, like the task force that would find rebel leaders and bring them in. "In to where?" the Board wondered, until Anna's deal with the army gave them access to a prison and other, less talked about means of getting information.

How do I know all of this?

I was there, in every meeting, typing notes on my tablet and blankly staring at the back wall during every lull in the conversation.

A human computer with good hair and a bespoke blue suit.

I wish I could say I would have eventually grown a conscience and quit, but that would be lying under oath.

I loved my job.

I loved the money that went into my account every two weeks.

I loved being a man-about-town with a limo and a driver and a different girl on my arm every night.

And look at me now.

Anyway, enough stalling. You asked me to tell you about Arrival Day, and I will—because I have to.

Arrival Day started out just like any other. I grabbed Anna's smoothie from the HealthCorp cafeteria and took it up to the top floor, where I poured it into a glass tumbler, added a metal straw, and tossed on a sprig of fresh mint from the plant on my windowsill. Since I had a black thumb, the mint plant was the twenty-second iteration of the original—but either Anna had never noticed the constantly dying plants, or she didn't care as long as that sprig floated in her drink every morning.

I carried the tumbler into her office on a round white tray with gold handles and set the whole thing by her elbow. She was on video chat and turned away from me, but she waved an arm as if to say, *Thanks, Tanner.* Her voice was calm and confident, but the way her hands squeezed her freshly painted red nails into her hands made me think she did not like whatever message the person on the other end was delivering. He had the look of a senator—old, white hair, red tie, American flag pin—and a voice that, even muted by Anna's headphones, seemed used to droning on about a topic while a bunch of other, equally boring old men waited for their turn at the microphone.

"Want a scone?" I mouthed.

She shook her head no. I tried not to look too relieved. The only scones Anna would eat were from Sylvia's, which was halfway across Manhattan. My phone rang from outside the office, and she waved me away, which meant I could sprint for the receiver before the last ring. I pressed the on button, and an unfamiliar face wearing a grey cap and sunglasses came on hologram.

"Hello, Anna Belore's office, how may I direct your call?" I asked.

There was a pop, pop, pop on the other end, and the man's face turned away from me. A movie on in the background? Fireworks? "How may I direct your call?" I repeated again, this time loud and slightly annoyed, as I hunched toward the phone and prepared to press the end button. The man's head whipped back.

"Tanner Coleman?"

I sat up straight. "Speaking. Who is this?"

"You don't know me, but I'm one of the guards downstairs. We are under a Code Red attack from enemy fire. I need to talk to Anna Belore immediately. I repeat, we are under—"

The call cut out.

I stared at the space in the air where the face had been.

"Anna?" I called out.

No reply. I swiveled my chair to see her through the open door. She was talking again, and she violently shook her head no at me, as if to say, *Now is not a good time.* I stood up on shaking legs and took two steps.

The rest seemed to happen in slow motion.

The elevator on the other end of the floor dinged. I turned my head without changing directions, and from the corner of my eye, I saw a green body and a furry body spring out. The green body was enormous, like a troll from an old fantasy movie; the furry body was decorated in some kind of shining battle armor. Both of them held standard issue HealthCorp guns. They shot at the row of public relations interns seated at their desks—Sarah with the ponytail, who died immediately; Amanda with the pixie cut, who turned and took the shot in her arm; Jacob with too much hair gel, who moaned for over ten minutes before bleeding out; and Dan with the empty briefcase, who pretended the shot hit him so he had an excuse to duck—and then through the glass at Marco, their manager, who required a second shot to fell him like a stubborn tree.

Then there was just Anna and I.

"What the fuck?" Anna yelled behind me.

Green troll and cat man advanced toward us. They walked with purpose but did not seem to be in a hurry. Whatever obstacles HealthCorp possessed had obviously been removed before these two made it to the top floor. As they came closer, I realized they were speaking English.

"What do you want?" I asked.

They examined me. I stared back. In my dreams, that moment, as I looked into the dust-colored eyes of the cat man and then up at the green troll's green eyes, which were darker at the irises but also green where the whites should have been, seems to last the whole night.

"Move aside," the green troll replied. Its mouth rolled the English words around and garbled them. "I have taken enough laffa for one day."

"What's laffa?" I stalled. My legs shook, but I managed to stay up and maintain my eye contact.

"Life," said the cat creature in much clearer pronunciation. "Your life. Now move, so that we may enact justice."

Behind me, a drawer closed. Then Anna's voice demanded, "Let him go." I turned slowly. She stood in the doorway with a HealthCorp gun drawn and her legs apart in a *Don't fuck with me, I've had official training* stance. For a second, I thought we were saved.

"Anna Belore," said the cat man in an official voice, as though he was reading a very formal court document, "you have been declared an enemy of the joint council of the Adalaffians and HoFe, now referred to as the HoFeLaffa. For your crimes, including the enslavement of our peoples, you have been sentenced to die."

I looked back at Anna, who seemed unsurprised by the strange words coming out of the creatures' mouths. Had she seen these creatures before? Did she know what the hell a "HoFe" was?

"Your people were a bunch of pathetic workhorses," she spit out with a vehemence that surprised even me, the frequent witness of her diatribes. Maybe she was scared after all. "What would you have done instead of work for HealthCorp? Weave some pretty baskets?"

The cat and the troll exchanged a flat glance. Then they began firing.

I found control of my body and jumped behind my desk. The impact broke my right arm and bruised my cheek, but I did not notice right away, since the exchange of bullets above my head distracted me. The shooting stopped, and then one pair of footsteps walked away from the scene. I could tell, after five years of hearing her heels on the luxury vinyl, that they were not Anna's.

The elevator dinged.

The survivor descended.

I used my good arm to raise my body up off the floor and looked around. Dan, who had also endured with a few scrapes, did the same. I took two steps and found the troll, who was face-down and oozing a slimy green juice, by my feet. As far as I could tell, he was dead—or at least close enough to it that he offered no threat. Past him, having fallen backwards from the doorway, was Anna, her face lax and strangely vulnerable in death.

"Is she…?" Dan asked.

I turned away from her and nodded.

"What do we do now?"

I adjusted my suit jacket and ran a hand through my hair. "Our jobs."

And we did them, for the three days between that first shooting and the fall of HealthCorp. Dan ran point on the press releases that went out from Anna's desk, and I spoke to the senators and security managers and lawyers.

On the fourth day, I left the office for the first time, went home, and packed a suitcase. I've been in New Jersey ever since.

Any more questions?

ARTICLE SEVENTEEN

Bina's Log

Your feet are red.

When you take a step, the pads stick to the cold floor. As you shift your weight, they peel, like slicing through a seaweed strand. The smell is unfamiliar but metallic. You think of your mother's cooking pot. And like food forgotten in that pot, the red crusts, forms streaks, stains.

"Wash, Bina."

The room with the red floor will be yours, along with the family who has adopted you. They have already removed the body, a sack in a plastic sheet, and cast it out into the sea without any laffas to put its soul to rest. Apparently, the seaweed has not pulled down the floating corpses, over a hundred of them, and so they bob away to the other side of Adalaffa. Even the planet itself has shunned them.

By the time the humans come back with fish nibbles in their skin, the command ship will be gone.

"Wash."

You dip the human shirt into the bucket and scrub at the blood. Dip. Scrub. Dip. Scrub. The water is red. Your hands are red. You wonder what would happen if the red blood touched your green, what color would that turn, what if you opened yourself and found out?

Dip.

Your mother's blood was blue.

Scrub.

Your mother is the reason you are on this ship.

Dip.

She would not have approved of all this death.

Scrub.

And yet she has caused it.

And yet again, you know that the death of Brayadin meant nothing to Tamalin or his three children. Not specifically. They were like the seaweed, just waiting for a splash above to send them lashing toward their prey.

But it meant something to you.

That is why you shot the man who used to sleep in this room.

####

His eyes were blue. Wide. White-framed. Afraid.

They reminded you of a planet you had never known.

Your mother used to say that Laffa was the heart of life. That when you opened your eyes in the morning and looked up through the open flap of your hut, you would see deedee birds in circular formations shooting past to new roosting locations and the spores of flowers twirling on the gentle breeze on their way to settle their many seeds. She used to say that laffa season lasted all year—that there was not a single day when laffa did not breed, and that, when she had arrived on Adalaffa, the emptiness of the lifeless sea had seemed as vast as the open sky.

Blue.

Wide.

####

Do you have a preference for where you put your mat? the family asks.

You don't.

Strange that the living quarters for one man will become the new home for four Adalaffians—with space to spare. The family decides to take his bunk and the space beneath as their sleeping space. You are given the strange little room where the man kept his extra uniforms. Your mat must be rolled at both edges, but you fit, your head and feet still a few inches from the walls. You have brought your blanket, an extra tunic and the one that had belonged to your mother, your clean pot, and a stirring spoon. All of these items also fit in the closet. You stay there as the family investigates the rest of the space and puts away the few signs of the man you killed: a photo of a woman, some white undergarments, a cup, the pile of uniforms. None of these will be discarded—Adalaffians know better than to waste good fabric—but they will be hidden, at least for a while. The family explains this and darts nervous glances in your direction.

While you wait for something to happen, rumors pass from door to door:

A few more humans have been found in the cafeteria.

Tamalin has figured out how to fly the ship.

The humans from the cafeteria have been killed and cast out into the sea.

Check the desk drawer. There's a special brown food in there that tastes even better than jam.

Tamalin is ready to leave.

The family tells you to come out of the closet. You don't. The family tells you to look out the portal window at Adalaffa for one last look at home. You don't. A vibration begins below you, like the small earthquakes that used to come before a tsunami. The family tells you this is it, we are leaving forever, it's okay because the new planet will provide more laffa for our people.

Don't feel sad. Don't cry.

You don't.

Space becomes the view from a window one foot in diameter. The view shifts, speckles with stars, blinds with sun, goes dark again. You know you should care more about it, but space feels like you do—cold and empty.

The family leaves for the cafeteria and returns with a strange concoction of foods. You will learn their names later—corn, peas, rice, beans—but on the tray they are just mountains of new colors. You think you should paint with them, not eat them.

Everyone stares at you. Two sets of blue eyes. One set of green eyes. You stare down at the tray and move the morsels of food from one compartment to another.

An hour later, the family leaves for a community meeting.

Finally, you stand and stretch your legs. You discover the concept of a restroom, a narrow tomb with a sink, showerhead, and strange white bowl that makes a terrifying whooshing sound when you press the silver button next to it. You pee into the hole in the floor instead of the bowl and avoid the button and run out before anything else can startle you.

Back in the room, you rifle through the items the family has brought with them. Same bowl, spoon, blankets, mats, and tunics as you, but also a stash of dried seaweed wrapped in a fourth mat and stored behind the desk. For what purpose?, you wonder. You slide one of the dried pieces from the pile and chew slowly on the end, which still has a little give—the texture of a piece of jerky, though you will learn this later when you access the commissary. The seaweed gives you a strange feeling of happiness, and for the first time, you feel grounded in your own body.

You are connected to Adalaffa, your mother used to say, but you know now that the connection is a physical tether, a deficiency. The seaweed is a drug, and you are in withdrawal.

You want to eat a second piece, but then Adalaffa will be one strand closer to gone. Your mother would tell you to ration.

You are your own mother now.

After the seaweed, you go back to your closet home and close the door against the space view. You have never sat in complete darkness before. Is this what your mother felt as she died? Is this the final step of laffa? When you hear the family coming down the hallway, you swing the door open and prop your feet up against the wall.

Voices pour in from the hallway, disappear with the close of the door. The family examines you and seems satisfied. The child, Jaydin, bounces around the room and onto the cot's mattress, off, on. They are two years younger than you, just eight years old, and yet filled with so much more laffa. Wait until we tell you, Jaydin keeps saying. Wait until you hear.

Hear what? you ask, the first words you have spoken since you entered this room. Your voice is high and a little shrill, like a whistle return.

The family explains that the Three Tams have assigned tasks to everyone onboard. Jaydin interrupts, And guess what? You're going to work as one of the command deck retrievers.

What does that mean?

Jaydin bounces, their hair a flapping brown bird against their chubby face. It means you get to see everything that happens up there! And retrieve stuff!

You shake your head. What stuff? And why me?

Jaydin shrugs. I guess your mother knew the Three Tams? I guess she was some kind of inspiration for them or something? Everyone has been talking about her. If she hadn't died, none of this—

Hush, says the woman. And you—she turns to you—you are to play an important role on this ship. To the people of Laffa. You must accept the work and perform it with honor. That is what Brayadin would want.

In your mind, you rage at her. What would you know about Brayadin? You think just because you brought her jam a few times you are connected to her in some special way?

But you also must admit that performing the work—any work—

with honor is exactly what your mother would want. Even sick, she continued to gather seaweed to earn Adalaffians a new world—one she knew she would never see. Even dying, she had reeled in the seaweed she had caught by the light of the moon so that you would have enough to fix their boat the next morning.

Even dead, she remains a giver of laffa.

####

The command deck is a bright light at the end of the hallway. You approach the entrance slowly, and no one notices you. The Adalaffian called Tamalin sits in a chair set up away from the lower level by a carpeted platform, his eyes frozen on the view of the black space in front of him. You have only seen him once before, the day the humans arrived on Adalaffa, but now he looks like a human in their uniform and the strange brown shoes on his feet. At least his hair has grown out, so that the brown shows in a line behind the blond.

The Three Tams sit at various stations around the room. The big twin—Bren?—is asleep, and Ven, the skinny twin with long hair, flips a knife and catches it. The third Tam, Sig, watches their father.

I would watch my mother that way, you think, if she came back from the dead.

"Yes?" Tamalin has noticed you. His face is somewhere between parent and elder. The way he looks down at you makes you feel like a laffafish at the end of a spear—or maybe that is just the effect of the raised platform.

"I'm Bina," you say.

"Brayadin's daughter," Ven explains without looking up from their knife.

"I see." Tamalin seems to examine you. "You're younger than I expected."

"We were mending boats and fishing at their age," says Sig. "I think they can fetch a cup of coffee."

You don't know the word "coffee," but you decide you like Sig best. You wonder if it was their idea to put you here, and what relationship they had to your mother. You never saw them together; then again, your mother only came to the boat to eat dinner and sleep. Perhaps they cared for her. Perhaps they—

"Did you hear me?" Tamalin asks.

"I'm sorry, I…"

"A biscuit. From the commissary. Please."

You turn and go back down the hallway you came from, though you are not even sure where it leads. Adalaffians pass you carrying brooms and buckets or speaking into little devices that seem to connect them to stations on the ship. "Tamalin said green is good," one of them says to someone on the other line. "As long as the light stays green, we can keep going." You end up running, doubling back, running in a perpendicular line, doubling back. The third time, you run into Sig, who grabs your shoulders to keep you from falling backward. The sharp beads at their chest have hurt your cheek, and you reach up to find blood there.

"Why did you pick me?" you ask. You feel like you might cry. "What did my mother mean to you?"

"Not her." Their hands are still at your shoulders. "You."

"I don't understand."

"A hundred humans were slaughtered on this ship, Bina. Only one of them was killed by a child." They look at you, really look at you, until you draw your eyes down to the floor. Then they let go of your shoulders. "Your mother's spirit lives inside of you, but you have your own laffa to lead. So do I."

Sig leads you back through the command deck. You feel tired, and you want to escape to your closet, but they tell you that running away won't solve the problem. "Don't say a word," Sig warns Ven as you pass, and they stay silent, though their eyebrows arch in what you suspect is mocking amusement. Bren is still sleeping. Tamalin watches, always watches, from the platform.

On the other side of the deck is another hallway, which branch-es into an identical maze of smaller hallways like capillaries from veins. While you walk, you ask Sig about their tattoos. "The story of our past, present, and future," Sig says. They point to a line of three planets hidden in a tangle of seaweed on their left forearm. "First Laffa. Then Adalaffa. Then…" They tap the third planet. "G11238P3."

"And you think our future is there?"

"I know our future is there. I just don't know what kind of future it will be."

You find the commissary, which is something like a store fit behind a single window through which an Adalaffian you do not recognize takes orders and gives people packaged food from the shelves behind them. "Adalaffians are rationed to one treat a day," Sig explains in a whisper, "but Tamalin can have as many as he wants."

You ask the Adalaffian for biscuits for Tamalin. "This is our new retriever," explains Sig. The worker hands over a yellow package, and when you run your fingers over the smooth wrapper, you feel a stack of four hard discs. You wonder what these biscuits taste like. Your mouth waters.

Sig takes you back a different way, a long way, that brings you back to the original quadrant of the ship where you were lost. "So we could have avoided going back through the command deck?" you ask angrily.

"And what lesson would that have taught you?"

The journey takes three weeks. A short time, but long when full of petty errands and day after day of biting your lips closed to keep from talking back. You learn the ship, and by the second week you can deliver a message to any Adalaffian on board—to the engineers down in the engine room, to the servers in the cafeteria, to the cleaners who dart around like laffafish sweeping and mopping your mess, and to the Three Tams in the hours when they are in their own quarters. Tamalin rarely leaves the command deck, and you often find him dozing while sitting completely upright, his hand always on the control panel at his arm. Such vigilance seems strange considering the ship seems to function on autopilot, but perhaps he still does not trust the humans, even in their death.

One afternoon, Tamalin sends you to Sig's quarters to ask him to announce a gathering.

You knock on their door, listen, and knock again.

"Come in," Sig says.

They are not asleep. In fact, they sit at their desk, identical to the one in the family's quarters, pouring over some documents in a foreign language. "You know English too?" you ask.

"Maybe." Sig closes the folder. "What does he want now?"

"A gathering." You keep looking at the folder.

"Of course. We're halfway there, and he needs to give everyone time to prepare."

"Prepare for what?"

Sig looks at you hard and then opens the folder. "This is the humans' report on G11238P3. From what I've translated so far, the planet is indeed similar to Laffa—abundance of oxygen from plant life, natural food sources, fresh water in the form of large lakes, everything we could hope for."

"And the problem?"

Sig taps the picture of the planet on their arm. "The problem is that unlike Laffa, G11238P3 did not have Laffians to control all of those aspects."

You come closer and touch your pointer finger to the image. Their skin is hot and turns a darker green at your touch. "So you're saying—"

"There is a reason the humans did not stop at G11238P3. They may have scrubbed that reason for their records," they point to a bunch of blacked out lines on the page, "but I suspect my father knows what it is."

You still do not understand. "Then why would he take us there?"

Sig closes the folder again and slams it down. "Because he knows what we do not—that the humans found over 12,000 galaxies on their way to us and gathered data on almost 500,000 planets. This one, this G11238P3, was the single other planet with life."

Laffa.

For the first time, the word carries fear.

What have you gotten yourselves into?

"It has come to my attention," says Tamalin to the crowd crammed into the cafeteria, "that the humans hid important information about our destination from us. They promised us a haven but gave us yet another Adalaffa. Only unlike our own planet…" He pauses for dramatic effect. You admire his blue jacket, something the humans call a blazer, with silver buttons that gleam in the harsh light of the room. "…something much worse than seaweed is waiting for us."

The crowd murmurs. A baby—the first one born on *The Santa Clara*, who they have thus named Columbin—cries and is comforted by their mother.

"What is worse than the seaweed?" asks one of the elders.

You know, from listening to Tamalin practice this speech during the hours when the Three Tams left him alone on the deck, that all these pauses are intentional. He wants the elders to ask questions. He wants to have all of the answers.

"The humans called the creatures *homo felis*." He sits down on one of the tables as though he is settling in for a story, and the rest of the Adalaffians follow suite, taking chairs where they can or finding space on the floor. "Though they do not seem to have interacted with these animals directly, their reports call them 'a humanlike animal that is half *primate*, half *feline*.'"

The crowd murmurs again. No one has heard of these strange words, and even from an Adalaffian's mouth, they sound like threats.

"Apparently, a *primate* is something like us—or like the humans— with large brains and long lifespans. They may move on two legs or four. They often live in trees. A *feline* is much like the Laffian *caldana*, only not an herbivore, so add claws and strong jaws and remove the sweet demeanor of the gentle, grazing *caldana*. So basically…" Tamalin leans forward. The crowd leans in too—even you, who knows better. "…smart, deadly monsters who will wipe us from G11238P3 within minutes of our arrival."

The crowd breaks into hysterics.

Jaydin, who is sitting near you, clutches at their mother and wails, "I don't want to go!"

You look around and catch Sig's eye; they wink at you as if to say *Didn't I tell you so?*

Right. This is all staged. You return your gaze to Tamalin.

"Do not panic." Your leader raises both hands in what you will learn, later, is the stance of the prophet. "All is not lost. For you see, I have a plan—one that will save us from the *homo felis* and grant us the planet the humans have promised. Would you like to hear it?"

As the crowd erupts in a cheer, you realize that Sig is gone.

"Something needs to be done about my father," Sig says the next time you are alone.

"What? When?"

"I am not sure." Sig shrugs. They do not seem upset, only thoughtful. "The moment will come, and we will know it."

####

That night, you dream of *homo felis*.

####

A day later you stand in Sig's quarters, this time to remind them of their shift on deck before you go to your closet to sleep. They hold a machine in their right hand—a gun, or at least some kind of weapon that takes the shape of one, though on closer inspection, there is a needle where the bullets should be. You stand near the door, silent. Your palms tingle.

"Come closer," says Sig.

You don't.

"Look." They place their left arm down on the desk and press the gun to their skin. Nothing happens. "This is how humans create tattoos."

You take a deep breath. Then you take two steps closer. "Are you adding one now?"

Sig removes the gun and places it delicately on the desk. "Actually, I thought you might want one."

They have read your thoughts again. But you cannot imagine what design you might place over your green canvas, for you have seen nothing but seaweed and laffafish your whole life.

"What about Brayadin?" Sig suggests.

You have not heard her name in many days, and the word startles you. Yes. Brayadin. "Can you tattoo a word?"

"You can tattoo anything," Sig says.

Brayadin. But you do not want the martyr. You want your mother. "What about Raya? That is what her parents called her."

"Put your arm on the desk and look away."

You do as you are told. Sig presses the needle to your forearm and moves their leg below the desk, where some kind of lever that controls the vibrations sends the gun into a frenzy. Your gaze stays on the window, on the darkness there, and then, as the view changes, on a single blinking star somewhere far in the distance. The vibrations tickle for a while, and then they begin to ache. You try to remember the last time you felt any physical pain. Was it the splinter in your finger from a dried seaweed piece? When one of the other children accidentally pushed you backward during a game of Chase the Fish? When your mother taught you to weave, and you could not sleep from the hurt of your hunched back?

But those instances of pain were different.

You did not like them.

But this pain…

The buzzing gets faster.

You smile.

The branding takes about half an hour. The buzzing is loud, and later, when you hear a bee for the first time, your arm will ache with the ghost of this memory. Neither of you speak. At the end, Sig tells you to look, and you see her name, Raya, written in a strange scrawl. It is Laffian, but the language is distorted, like looking at the word under water.

"I wrote it in the design of a piece of split seaweed," Sig explains. They point to the middle between the first two letters and last.

"To remind me to make my own path from hers?" you ask.

Sig touches your face gently and wipes, and you are surprised to find their fingers wet. "You won't need a reminder."

####

Every Adalaffian of age is issued a weapon and a time slot in the training room in which to learn how to use it. As Tamalin's assistant, you distribute these schedules throughout the ship. Most of the Adalaffians seem eager to learn, but yet disappointed that until they do, they will not have the opportunity to hold one of the black guns the humans cared so much about. *The last thing we need is four hundred Adalaffians running around shooting each other*, Sig had said when they insisted on the schedule and training. *Of course. But they must be able to defend themselves and their families*, Tamalin had said. *The minute we land, we will be at war.*

War. You repeat this human word to yourself. Sig tells you it means the opposite of "Unity in Laffa"—that it means the opposite of laffa in general. "Kill or be killed," they say.

If this is the system of logic on Earth, it sounds like a very dangerous place.

During the distribution of the schedules, you stumble upon a family reciting the fifty laffas of a funeral service. You cannot see the body, but you recognize the special robe the elder wears and the way the people in the room have crowded around the bed. Before you can back out of the room, everyone has noticed you.

"Yes, child?" asks the elder.

"Nothing. Just the training notice for the people of age in this household."

"Leave them on the desk," says an older Adalaffian with tears in their eyes. "But no need to leave one for Muradin."

You slip Muradin's sheet into your tunic pocket and drop the next two on the desk for the spouse and additional child over fifteen.

####

They are peaceful sleepers, but heavy ones. After what feels like an hour you crack open the door, where the room looks bright by comparison. Three bodies, all cocooned in their blankets and facing away from you. Three bodies, breathing slowly.

You tiptoe past them and out the door to the hallway, where you consider your shoes but then leave them behind. Better not to make a sound. The training room is far, but you know that only one guard is awake to patrol the halls on either side of the ship at night. Before you turn down every hallway, you bob your head out and check for signs of life. The first guard sits on a desk chair in front of their own door drinking a mug of that black liquid from the cafeteria, so you simply go the longer way around. The second guard is actually patrolling, but the wrong direction, so that you can go halfway down the hall and turn out of sight without their gaze ever falling on you.

Finally, the training room.

It is a small room, and empty besides a desk with a charging station, headset, and plastic weapon on top and a rack of hanging bags on one side. You place Muradin's training sheet in the pile on the desk and take up the strange black equipment there. By pressing on every spot on its surface, you eventually find the on button and push. Then you take up the plastic weapon and, with your other hand, place the headset over your head.

You are in the forest.

Light filters through the large leaves and shows you the ground at your feet, littered with leaves of red, brown, and gold. There are patches of grass there, too, and gray rocks. Bird calls echo and distract. A stick breaks somewhere out of sight. Your mother told you of this place, where as a child she chased her siblings in endless games of Chase the Fish—though, back on Laffa, this game was called Catch the Sefers.

If only she were here.

Suddenly, a faceless figure runs at you from behind a tree. Before you can even think, you raise the weapon and fire. A boom sends a bullet into the arm of your attacker, and a second kills them with a chest wound. The body fades and then disappears, leaving no imprints in the leaves.

"Well done," says a voice from high above. The voice is robotic, but at least it speaks Laffian. Who programmed it, and how? "When aiming, you always want to focus on the central mass of your target. Remember, your weapon holds fifteen bullets, after which you will need to reload. For a demonstration, please press the button on the left ear of your headset. Otherwise—"

You press the left button.

The forest fades and in its place a woman appears floating in space. She looks a lot like Captain Rosa, only she wears a nondescript uniform that is much tighter than the standard issue and seems to have accentuated sexual features. "When reloading your gun, place the flat part of the magazine against the palm of your hand." A gun appears in her hand and she demonstrates. "Place a round on top and press down so that the round loads into the magazine. Fill the magazine with fifteen rounds, one on top of the other, and then slide the magazine back in the handgun. Push on the slide lock and aim." The gun in her hand disappears. "If you would like to repeat these instructions, please press the left button again. To return to target practice, please press the right button or wait five seconds for—"

You press the right button.

The forest reappears.

You raise the plastic gun and prepare to fire.

####

"You look tired," Jaydin says the next morning.

"I haven't been sleeping well." Quickly, you gulp down a mug of coffee and enjoy the buzz of instant energy. "And Tamalin's been working me hard."

"You're so lucky." Jaydin frowns at their mop, which is propped against the wall nearby.

"That's one word for it."

You hide a yawn in your hand and return for another cup of coffee.

####

Seven days until landing. Six nights of training. You hide your gun in one of your mother's tunics in the corner of the closet and sleep with one hand touching the pile.

####

You grow so accustomed to holding the gun all night that without it, your hand shakes.

####

On the last night, you finish the practice course in under three minutes.

####

The Santa Clara approaches G11238P3.

You are lucky you are on duty in the command deck, which means you have the best view. The sphere enlarges and becomes textured in the front window. The land is rolling but not mountainous; the bodies of water are large but not sea-like. Clouds drift over the surface but do not threaten.

"Beautiful," Sig says. No one else says anything. Likely, they are thinking of war—and of death.

An hour later, the lens of your view zooms in again, revealing thick green forests and expanses of grassy plains.

"The planet seems so peaceful," Sig says.

"Don't be a fool," Tamalin retorts. "Do you know how peaceful Adalaffa looked from space?"

An hour later, you land in the middle of one of the wide-open plains.

"All armed Laffians, prepare to disembark," orders Tamalin over the intercom. "Take only your weapons and your standard issue communicators. All unarmed citizens are to wait on *The Santa Clara* until further instructions." He turns to you. "That means you too, Bina. Stay with your family and wait."

You nod and scamper back to your room. Armed citizens push through the halls in the opposite direction, toward the ramp that will spit them and their gunfire onto G11238P3. Someone accidentally elbows you in the side, and someone else shoulders you so hard you spin a little before regaining your balance. The people are scared and violent, you remind yourself as you push through the last of them and find your room number, but you are not comforted; besides when you took over *The Santa Clara* that bloody day, those two words had never applied to Adalaffians before.

The family is crammed at the portal window. "Can I see, too?" you ask, and Jaydin makes a little space for you. "Seen anything yet?" Jaydin shakes their head no. All of you nervously press forward, your bodies full of the same adrenaline and fear as the Adalaffians soon to embark on their first journey on G11238P3.

There.

In the trees.

Those blurs.

Homo felis.

More of them press out from the space between the trees and form a crowd, giving you a good view of their compact, furry bodies. They are the color of sand dredged from the bottom of Adalaffa, an earthy tan. They stand upright and share the same general body shape as Adalaffians, though you suspect close-up they are shorter. Some kind of armor shields their sexual features. They have small, pointy ears on the top of their heads and delicate pink noses; their hands are paws, large and clawed, and so are their bare feet. When one turns, a tail swishes up and whips like a drying cloth left hanging in the wind.

They are also armed.

In fact, as they come closer, you realize their weapons are the same as the ones the Adalaffians commandeered from the humans. How did the same guns end up on a planet the humans never set foot on? And why would the humans have promised you a planet they knew, for a fact, was already inhabited by intelligent lifeforms?

Whatever the reasons, you suspect Tamalin knows them.

You slip back into a memory. A ship descends from the sky, bringing roar and spray to the otherwise always undisturbed water. Creatures much like Adalaffians appear. You cling to your mother's waist and bury your head in her tunic. A ramp descends, drawing your attention back again, and one of you neighbors leaps on and disappears into the belly of the ship.

A few years later, your mother is dead.

Are there *homo felis* children holding their mothers' hands in those trees?

You have to go. You run to the closet and throw the tunics in the air until you find the right one, then slide the gun into your pocket. "Where are you—?" "What are you?—" voices ask behind you, but then you are out the door and sprinting down the now-empty hallway. Left, right, left. You zigzag across the ship until you are across, at the ramp, which has already released the Adalaffian troops and rests waiting on the tall grass for their victorious return. The air smells like the herbs in the cafeteria packets. Your breath comes in effortful gasps.

When you reach ground level, you find them not far ahead of you, just a few hundred feet. They move slowly, guns up, toward the *homo felis*, who are doing the same. You slip the gun behind your back and run again, this time the longer way, around the side of the crowd. More and more *homo felis* leave the trees, forming a force at least as large as the Adalaffians. They are all going to die.

Finally, you get ahead of the group and spot Tamalin and the Three Tams leading the front lines.

"Halt!" orders Tamalin. All of the Adalaffians stop at once, and one of the leaders of the *homo felis* must shout something similar, because their troops do the same.

During this moment, your eyes meet Sig's. *Your own laffa*, they mouth, or at least that is what you imagine, since they tap their forearm—the place where your tattoo still aches—with the front of their gun.

You kneel in the tall grass.

You whisper "For laffa" as you raise your weapon.

You fire.

ARTICLE EIGHTEEN

Homo Felis: The Hidden Story

of Our First Encounter

Written by Dennis Lus and Mark Lake

Produced by the Society for the

Wellness of HoFeLaffian Teens

SCENE ONE

FADE IN:

EXT. THE PLANET HOFE - EARLY MORNING

The suns rise, revealing two human explorers in
tan camouflage hiding behind a large boulder. The

humans are in the desert facing a thick line of
trees. DENNIS, a middle-aged Southerner with salt
and pepper hair and beard, holds the binocu-
lars; LUCA, young and strong with muscles bulging
against his shirt, holds the camera.

                    DENNIS

          Whatdaya reckon?
          Are we in danger
          here, Luca?

                     LUCA

          Nah. Bunch of big
          domestics, that's
          all. Remind me of
          my son's cat Dip-
          sy.

                    DENNIS

          I got a cat, too.
          Scratched the liv-
          ing crap outta me
          before I left just
          for petting her
          belly. I tell you,
          Luca, I'm nervous
          as hell.

                     LUCA

          That's what I'm
          here for.

Luca RAISES his gun. Just then, a HoFe EMERGES

from the forest wearing a breastplate and spear on his back. His hair is tan with streaks of white. He appears older, though still agile.

                    LUCA

          You getting this,
          Dennis?

                    DENNIS

          Yessiree.

                    LUCA

          (squints) Wait a
          minute. What's he
          doing? Oh God,
          he's going to—

The men LOOK around the boulder. Luca SHOOTS the attacking HoFe and MISSES. The HoFe TACKLES him to the ground and IMPALES Luca with ten sharp claws. Dennis PICKS UP the fallen gun and SHOOTS. He WOUNDS the HoFe. Blood spurts all over him. (This scene should be very overly dramatic. Blood should continue to spurt long after it makes sense to do so.)

                    DENNIS

          That's what you
          get for messing
          with the strongest
          species in the
          cosmos.

Dennis looks far into the distance as the HoFe
runs away.

                    DENNIS (like a cowboy)

                    Run, little kit-
                    ty cat, while you
                    still can. But
                    mark my words:
                    I'm gonna come
                    back for you—and
                    I'm gonna bring
                    some of my friends
                    along for the
                    ride, too.

SCENE TWO

Final image of dying Luca at the end of Scene One is frozen on the screen.

                    DENNIS (V.O.)

                    That scene prob-
                    ably looked like
                    the story you've
                    read about in the
                    history books,
                    huh, kids? The
                    truth, however, is
                    another matter en-
                    tirely.

The scene rewinds. The men are back behind the rock. The HoFe finds a sunny spot on a nearby rock and takes off his spear and breastplate. After a while, some dusty critters run over his legs; he is not bothered. He yawns; he stretches. His ears perk and relax. He falls asleep.

                    LUCA

                    He's snoring. Come
                    on, let's get a
                    closer look.

                    DENNIS

                    I don't think—

                    LUCA

          We can't go back
          without a tro-
          phy, Dennis. A
          few rusty rocks
          and some leaf sam-
          ples are not going
          to put us on the
          front page.

                   DENNIS

          True. But I'd
          rather be ignored
          than dead.

                    LUCA

          Suit yourself.

Luca CROUCHES and then begins to ARMY CRAWL toward
the sleeping HoFe. Dennis shakes his head and then
FOLLOWS him.

When they get about ten feet away, one of the
HoFe's eyes OPENS. He SAYS something indistin-
guishable. Before the two men can run, he seizes
his spear and IMPALES it in Luca's chest.

Dennis FALLS into a worshipping bow on the ground.
His whole body is shaking.

The HoFe RISES to his full height, shorter than

Dennis's but taller when combined with the boulder. His paws RAISE and REVEAL sharp claws. He
JUMPS off the boulder and retrieves his spear from
Luca's dead body, which makes a terrible SQUISH
sound. Dennis LOOKS UP at him.

                    DENNIS

          Please don't kill
          me. I wasn't real-
          ly gonna let him
          shoot you. Honest.

The HoFe gives Dennis a stern and knowing glance.
Then he TURNS away, falls to ALL FOURS, and DISAP-
PEARS back into the forest.

ARTICLE NINETEEN

Official Order for the Continuation of the Special Council

September 1, 2140

The Council of Elders has deemed it necessary to extend the Special Council's adjudications for a period greater than five years and no longer than twenty. We apologize for any inconvenience this delay causes, and ask, again, for your patience.

ARTICLE TWENTY

From the Lectures of Professor Agi

Welcome to HoFeLaffian Earth Law for Humans. My name is Professor Agi, and I will be your instructor for the semester. I've been teaching this course, as well as HoFeLaffian-Human Relations, for over ten years, since the first course on such subjects was ever introduced to your college curriculum, and I will still be here teaching it when your children apply for their spots.

As is standard in my classes, we will be discussing topics that are not necessarily "in the books." Ever since the HoFeLaffians arrived here on Earth, we've been doing our best to blend into the fabric of your world. Mentioning the old ways is all but forbidden. However, on this, the first day of class, I'm going to do the unthinkable: I'm going to tell you about my planet. Specifically, I'm going to tell you about the day the Laffians arrived.

I see you're excited.

I see you're nervous that I'll get in trouble.

Well, listen up, children: I won't. And do you know why?

Because I'm an elder.

And this word, "elder," brings us right back to where we started: my planet. See, on HoFe, the elderly were treated much like yours— thought to be senile, often ignored. Over the years, they grew weaker and weaker; their eyesight declined. It was not until the arrival of the Laffians that the respectful category of "elder" entered our lexicon—and that's understandable, when you consider the HoFe are a warrior species.

Wait.

Let me leap back.

Let's start with that name: HoFe. Do you know that a long time ago, before the humans arrived on our planet, we were called Cye? Let me write that word on the board. Cye. The name of my people; a name almost forgotten.

Wait.

One leap back again.

Do you know that we're not cats?

That word, "felis," was another one of your brilliant contributions. Your explorers saw a warrior species, strong as your lions and fast as your cheetahs, and thought, *You know what would be a really original name for an alien race that could rip our throats out in less time than it takes us to load a gun? Cats!* And then, with your typical hubris, you tacked on that other word, "homo," as if there was anything connecting your pea-sized brains to the immensity of what sits behind our broad, furred foreheads.

But I digress.

A few more details about us: first, we do not have claws on our bottom paws, which we use only for walking. We do not have silky pink tongues either. I will admit that we do have pink noses and pointy ears, as a previous testimony conveyed and as those of you in this room can clearly see on my head. Our tails are also long like your cats, and they do flick, swish, and wave. At the moment the Laffians arrived, they were mostly lashing, which served as an added distraction for our enemies should they try to aim from a great distance. Our strong hind legs tensed in anticipation. As an arthritic HoFe holding a few extra pounds—what I tell the children is the weight of my wisdom—I planned to stay back during these maneuvers and then surprise the invaders from below my leaping leaders. I am not ashamed of these traits; however, I do understand that they change your perception of me.

Wait. You'll need to know a bit more about our history for this story to make any sense.

In summary, the Cye were once comprised of two groups: the Cye-Ma and the Cye-Ra. The Cye-Ma were our healers, gatherers who mixed medicines and invented new ways of healing, such as the Cye practice of ingesting our own guard hairs as calcium supplements. If you look here at the projector, Image A is a Cye-Ma female carrying a basket of herbs.

The Cye-Ra were our warriors, fighters who rid our lands of all of the other predators who had evolved along with us, such as the Wo, which I can only describe in your language as a bear the size of a truck and with the jaw of a great white. Not at all accurate, but you felt a stab of fear right through your tiny little hearts, didn't you? Image B is a Cye-Ra spear.

Are you wondering, dear students, why this is the first you're hearing of the Cye-Ma and Cye-Ra?

Why, it's because you killed them all.

Well, that's not really true. You killed enough to make the separate names, Cye-Ma and Cye-Ra, irrelevant.

I was there that day, you know. Just a small kitten—kidding, kidding—who was helping his father tend to a wound from a tenacious Jep who had taken a chunk out of the Cye-Ra General's right arm with its sharp canine teeth. Our generals stand at the front of the battle line, by the way, in case there was any doubt. So I was there, literally at his right hand, when the first humans arrived.

I was there when they shot down our whole line of defense like your children shooting bottles in a carnival game.

Bam-bam-bam-bam-bam.

Sorry for startling you, front row. The desk pounding was probably unnecessary.

Let's get there a different way. Have you ever smelled blood? Now try imagining that metallic scent multiplied by a thousand and intensified by 400 million odor sensors.

You understand, now, why the Cye-Ma allowed the humans to enslave us. We were not warriors. We had not picked up spears since our Division Day as children. And what chance did we have, the weakest of our line, against the strength of your guns and the magic of your ships?

Now let's see…

I was telling you all of this for a reason…

Right. I was explaining why elders were not respected on HoFe, and how that concept, of wisdom with age, was a true gift from our new friends, the Laffians. But around and around we go. Such is the thought pattern of an elder.

I was there that day too, you know. When the Laffians arrived. I was an old man already, but not so old as I am now, and my eyesight was clear as a calm lake. I was there that day, as I said, dressed in my heavy metal breastplate, and the sun kept me warm even as the human ship once again descended to try to claim what was ours.

What was that?

The breastplate?

Right, I missed a step. I tend to do that—to jump from A to C. Call me out on it, okay? Let me know.

After we chased the humans off, we—

What?

Oh! Right! I forgot to tell you how we got them to leave. Do you know, it was all those predators I mentioned? We caught them in cages, starved them, and then, right at their hungriest, we released them right at the doors of the human's temporary armory. The humans had moved them out of their ship, the guns, in order to give them easy access—as I said, tiny little brains—and had left only five guards to watch the whole place.

They underestimated us—and now that I see what scholars on your planet look like, I understand why.

I jest.

Not really.

Don't tell the other professors, okay?

So we ran off the humans, and then we ran off the last of our planet's beasts, and then we began to train. The few Cye-Ra elders—See, there's that word again—remaining helped us learn the ways of our lost clan and improve them.

We became unstoppable.

So there I was, a member of our Cye army—which was now called our HoFe army, by the way, because we all spoke the more elaborate language of English—my breastplate warming in the sun, when the Laffi-ans came down in that shiny ship they'd stolen. Naturally, we assumed the humans had come back for our hofellium, and we were prepared to defend it until the last HoFe fell dead on the field.

Have you seen it, by the way? The hofellium?

No?

I suppose you wouldn't say, considering hofellium flakes are now illegal. For good reason, by the way—those things will make you see stars, and not in the fun way. A lot of good students have died from it.

Anyway, you can picture a red metal nugget, smooth and oblong with lighter red etches where the elements and the HoFe have kicked and dug and pressed on it. Picture a human heart, for that is what Captain Rosa said as she held one of the nuggets up to the light like a murderous god. Oh, how those red nuggets captivated them, the red nuggets we called a nuisance for the way they poisoned the roots of our crops.

Believe it or not, in our youth, my sister and I used to use the hofellium nuggets as balls and pitch them back and forth with nets attached to long sticks.

Where was I?

Thank you. The second human ship.

It landed on one of our dead fields, which the humans called our hofellium beds but which we called ghost lands in honor of the many dead harvests put to rest there. Not that we were too bitter—HoFe was a plentiful planet, and we could always gather and hunt what we needed from the forests—but we had hoped to create a system that would leave us time for leisure. Looking back, I cannot recall what that leisure was, and likely, we had no actual plans.

Maybe we just wanted to sleep more. That part of our "felis" categorization is accurate. Do you know that my uncle once slept for fifty-two hours straight, and that even a bucket of water over his head did not wake him? Fifty-two hours, and after all that time, he slid his eyes open and asked, tail twitching playfully, what my aunt had prepared for dinner. Dinner! Can you believe it? It was the middle of the night two days later!

What did you say?

The human ship?

Right. I apologize. You see, my mind drifts these days, and I often feel like a leaf in the wind that never comes to rest. But I will rest, one day soon, and…

But I'm getting off topic again.

I looked across the field and shuddered. As I said, I had been there the first time, when *The Santa Clara* landed; I had felt the dust blown from their ship and felt the awe of a believer facing a god. I had watched our people fall in the fields as one by one they became the true ghosts of that cursed land and felt true shame. Now, the human ship had returned, and this time, we were ready.

We were prepared to die.

The HoFe warriors came from the forest like a flock and proceeded forward. Triggered by our adrenaline, our fur rose and hardened, creating, if not a shield, then a deflector. If their bullets came at the right angle, they would bounce off or fall. Our claws extended into twelve short knives. Most importantly, we held the guns we had taken from the humans, but we also kept our old spears, still our preferred hunting tools, strapped to our backs.

Guns. Spears. Claws. Shields.

We were prepared to die, but we would fight to live.

My left paw crossed my chest to rest on my spear. My mother, who was a great healer, had cut its mother branch from her parents' tree and carved a mosaic of leaves. When she passed the spear to my brother, one of the defeated Cye-Ra, she had said, *May you be quiet as wind through leaves, yet deadly as the gusts that fell them.* Even after my brother's death, my mother still believed strongly in the Cye-Ma concept of fighting only when absolutely necessary—a belief that many of us still shared, even if we were willing to put that view aside for a while.

What?

Oh. I forgot already. We were talking about the Laffians. I mean, the Adalaffians. Goodness, these names do confuse.

Anyway, our assailants descended from the ramp. They had green and blue bodies, tall and thin compared to ours, and my first thought was that the whole of them was like the splayed feathers of the peacocks we'd seen in the human translator—ironic, considering that I now know that Adalaffians all look strikingly similar.

By the way, it is quite strange that your people call something with such a clear name—in this case, peafowl—a completely different name. Peafowl seems more accurate. I think I shall use it from this point on. Another interesting fact about peafowl is that they orient their courtship displays toward the sun to enhance the look of their eyespot feathers.

How did I get on this topic?

Of course.

The Adalaffians.

In many ways they were more human than we were, and if not for their coloring, we would likely have attacked without thinking twice. As it happened, they drew their weapons anyway, leaving us no choice but to go on the defensive. We pressed forward, and they pressed forward, and we became two sides of a bar clamp until the space between us was just a thousand feet. They were here for the hofellium, most likely—or worse, for us—and they seemed prepared to die to get their target. Their leader stood front and center, obvious for his human uniform and the orders he called out in a strange language, and we all knew without an order that he would be killed first.

We all raised our guns.

I thought of my poor wife, one of the rare healers still allowed to practice medicine, who would down a draught of poison and be dead before our enslavers stepped foot in our dwelling. She had told me so herself; she had showed me the red bottle, which she kept hanging above the bed so that it blinked like a firefly when it caught candlelight—or like the candles we lit at our coupling ceremony, which my father had made from his own wax and kept in tall jars to protect the flames from the wind. Superstition says that a candle that blows out before morning means a short coupling, but our candle flickered well into the next day, or so my father said. How this all brings me back—and to the way Sora looked as she stood facing me, small flowers threaded into the fur around her face and laced into her braid and tail, dress swaying in the breeze, as though the wind had picked her up with the petals and stems and carried her right to me. I'll never forget her, my wind-waved flower, my candle flame steady against the breeze.

Where was I?

Right. I was about to fire. I thought of her, and I aimed, and I prayed, not that my volley would save us, but that the sound might serve as a warning to the people to take their own guns in hand.

Then a shot fired from their side, somewhere off to our right and definitely not part of our forces, and their leader fell.

The field descended into chaos.

Our side split and turned, so that we ended up circling and retreating to a safer distance. One of my fellow HoFe knocked me down—or maybe it was my own feet—and then another soldier took me by the armpits and hoisted me back up. Embarrassing, to say the least, but at least I didn't get trampled to death. Had the Adalaffians thought to fire at us then, they could have killed most of us with easy shots at our backs. Not that they noticed! They crowded around their fallen general like frightened ducklings around their mother and called out two words over and over again: *laffa* and *Tamalin*. We knew then that these were no warriors, and our tense bodies relaxed into poses of curiosity. Our tails swished low to the ground.

Eventually, the Adalaffian who had fired the shot was brought to the center of the line. They were of an indistinct sex, but most definitely a child. One of the general's advisors, a bald one with strange markings on their skin, seemed to be arguing with the two others—one large like the most overweight of our elders and one with very long hair—about the child's actions. The child looked off somewhere in the distance between our two forces, their expression blank and unseeing. In HoFellian, we would call such an individual "ghost ridden," but in English, you would probably describe them as "psychologically traumatized."

In the midst of this confusion, the wounded general, who seemed to be not dead after all, was carried back onto the ship.

After more arguing, the bald creature with the markings dropped their gun in the grass and walked toward us with their hands in the air. Our leader, General Fah, met them, though he did not drop his weapon. Fool me once…

By the way, have I mentioned that General Fah is my second cousin on my mother's side? The first of our family to achieve a military rank of such caliber, he was always the favorite of the family, though as a child we mocked him for the drills he completed at the base of the tree, often with the use of a sharp stick and a—

Who?

General Sig?

Right. He met General Fah on the field between our forces, but closer to our lines, so that we could hear them. Unlike General Fah, Sig—who, of course, was just plain Sig at the time—walked with a casual saunter, as though they were meeting General Fah on a stroll and not on a battlefield where our people had died for HoFe already and were prepared to die again. This attitude did, however, convey its own kind of confidence, and I felt there was something dark and dangerous inside of them.

"*Holaffa*," said Sig.

"I am General Fah," said General Fah in English with an accompanying pounding of his chest. "If you can understand me with the use of some kind of translator, please explain quickly why you are here." He kept his gun aimed, and his tail lashed menacingly against the special uniform stitched with a HoFe warrior in strands of hofellium that marked him as our leader. Though I could not see his face, I imagined it as a snarl.

"You speak English?" said Sig in awkward but understandable English. "This is a surprise."

General Fah took the crouched stance of an attack. "How do you know the words of our enemies?"

"General, I suspect you and I have more in common than you think," Sig said with a smile. Then they placed a hand of brotherhood on General Fah's shoulder. "Why don't we call a truce and talk about it?"

For over an hour, the troops waited on the battlefield. The weather was a cool eighty degrees—a typical spring day on HoFe—but would likely reach a moderate hundred before the sun began its descent. Glints of orange bedded in the ground like potatoes revealed the hiding places of smaller nuggets of hofellium, the ones the humans had not had the chance to melt down and turn into bullets or edible flakes.

Do you find it as strange as I do that those two products are Health-Corp's largest moneymakers?

Anyway, back to the day in question. The Adalaffians, who seemed to tire more easily, sat on the ground in small circles. They lifted their tunics off their chests to dry their sweating foreheads. We, trained in the daily maneuvers required of every citizen, remained upright and armed. Still, we whispered among us, wondering where they had come from, how they knew English, and most importantly, what they wanted from us.

Time seemed to stand still.

In our language, we have many different words for these kinds of pauses. There is a word that means a calm and serene pause, and a word that means a lethargic pause. The pause of the kind I am describing on the battlefield is a special pause that means "a pause due to fear and worry."

The HoFe reaction is always to freeze and wait.

Yet I consider myself an interesting case study, because that day I did not freeze and wait, even under direct orders from General Fah. Instead, I ambled over to the place where General Fah and Sig sat on two large boulders and took a seat on a smaller rock at the foot of Fah's stone. The two leaders did not even notice me, so deep in conversation were they about the humans who had enslaved us both, until I found a small pause, which is a different word again, in which to interrupt.

"Excuse me, General."

General Fah looked down at me and glared. "What is it, Agi?"

I mentioned that General Fah is my second cousin on my mother's side, didn't I? And about the sharp stick? Yes, I suppose I did—well, my point is that even though he wore the uniform of a general, I could never quite get the image of little cousin Fah out of my mind. Our genetic link made me bolder than the other soldiers—more prone to offer my feedback on his training exercises, for example, or on the need for live animals on which to practice our shots, or… well, perhaps I went too far. I only wanted to be helpful, and to give the HoFe the best chance for survival. No wonder, though, that he often turned and hurried in the opposite direction when I approached.

"Well, Fah—"

"General Fah," he corrected.

"Right, General Fah. I felt it my duty to point out that—"

"Your duty is to stand in line and wait for my orders," he pointed out.

"Yes. Of course. But I couldn't help thinking that these—uh—what are you, exactly?"

"Adalaffians," said the green creature.

"—that these Adalaffians," I pressed on, "have been maltreated by the humans just as we were, not too many years ago. Perhaps, if we allow them to stay here for a short time, we might help them recover and then find a suitable planet for their habitation."

General Fah and Sig shared a smile. "A brilliant plan, Agi," said Fah. "Thank you for your input. Now, if you would return to the ranks so that the other soldiers do not feel set apart, that would be most helpful."

When General Fah finally returned with Sig, he did so with his gun lowered and holstered and his arm held up to our troops as a sign that peace had been made.

"These people are our brothers in bondage," General Fah announced to our troops. I felt proud about my part in the reconciliation, but I tried not to look too smug about it. "The humans have also exploited them to make a profit off their resources. We will offer them temporary respite as refugees until a decision can be made about their fate. None of them are to be harmed. Understood?"

"Understood, General!" we replied.

We holstered our own weapons and stood at ease.

####

But where to put them?

HoFe dwellings were not a possibility. We built our homes in the tops of the tallest trees, quite similar in height and design to your tropical Kapok trees, up which we climbed on all fours using thin ramps without railings. These ramps were too close together to accommodate the Adalaffians' upright height, and too dangerous without holds for their weak and clawless hands. We were also accustomed to doing thrice daily sweeps of our dwellings for the deadly creatures who might attempt residence—venomous spiders, venomous snakes, and poisonous *branaynays* similar to frogs but with only two legs that carry venom in their sticky feet—as well as remaining knowledgeable in quick healing poultices should an injury occur. If the Adalaffians came up into the trees, we explained, they would likely halve their numbers within a week.

You should have seen their faces when they heard about *branaynays*.

Not that they understood us directly, of course. It seemed that the wounded Tamalin, their offspring Sig, and the child who had fired the gun were the only ones who spoke English on *The Santa Clara*. The rest of the people had use of the humans' translators, however, and these machines, having first spent time on our planet, could turn both human and HoFellian words into Adalaffian.

"What skills do your people have?" asked General Fah.

Sig explained about the planet Adalaffa, which had about the same effect on us as the prospect of poisonous *branaynays* had on their people. An entire planet covered in water? With deadly seaweed that could pull a grown creature down into its depths? We shuddered. The rain in our forests and the rare trips to the lakes for fish were already unpleasant enough.

"This weaving," mused General Fah. "Do you think it would work with fibers from the fronds of our palm trees?"

We brought a small contingency of the Adalaffians into the forest only long enough to point out what elements they needed. Our people had never even seen a basket—paws and claws are not exactly conducive to delicate handiwork—and thus, we needed their guidance to explain what to collect. They seemed especially interested in the palm fronds, green outer leaves ten feet in length and comprised of fifteen smaller two-foot-long leaves, as well as kapok branches, which they might use for rods.

At one point, a young Adalaffian happened to attract a beetle during a leaf inspection, and they screamed so loudly that birds exploded from their nests. "A branaynay!" they exclaimed, hitting their arms. "Help!"

"That beetle is venomous, not poisonous," I said, clapping them on the back. "As long as it didn't bite you, you should be fine."

That poor Adalaffian rushed off to check his body for bite marks, leaving me no time to confess that I had been only teasing about the beetle. How serious they are, I thought as I hurried to catch up with the group.

The Adalaffians' eyesight seemed reduced, or perhaps they were just accustomed to not seeing anything but water, because they stumbled frequently. A rock? Trip. Soft earth? Trip. A tree root? Sprawled out on the ground and potentially sprained arm.

"I think we have the information we need," General Fah said delicately once some fronds and branches had been collected. "Why don't your people return to your ship to rest?"

Had the visitors been HoFe, they would have stubbornly refused the help. Instead, they agreed that rest was called for, and even allowed a guide to take them back through the forest instead of trying to backtrack on their own! How logical; how foreign. They, disappearing into the trees in synchronous step, were like one organism, while we wrestled and chased off our energy. Not me, of course—I had found a nice stump on which to rest my weary haunches, and I now licked at a cut on my arm from my fall.

"No time to rest," General Fah said as he came up behind me. "We have work to do."

Though we had already been long on our feet, General Fah set us to gathering palms and rods, which we piled outside of the forest for easy access. While we gathered, we talked.

"We almost killed them all."

"Is that why the humans planned to bring them here?"

"It's like the story of the snake in the branaynay nest."

"Or the story of the branaynay in the ant chamber."

"It's like that time that Balaylay asked his twin brother to go fishing for him because he knew the husband of his mistress was waiting at the lake."

"You're right!"

One thing you should know about the HoFe is that we are storytellers. Not only do we have an extensive collection of myths, but we also like to exaggerate, so that even an event that happened an hour before becomes legend almost immediately. We also hate busywork, so the stories keep our minds occupied while our hands do the gathering.

Anyway, we gathered until the sun went down, and then we returned home. My back was already bordering on arthritic, and I struggled to climb the ramp up my tree, pausing several times to take some deep breaths and arch my back against the discomfort of the climbing hunch. During these pauses I admired the flashing of a bug much like your firefly in hanging in nets in the nearby houses, as well as the free insects lower down the tree bobbing and weaving through the lower branches. In general, the HoFe preferred the dim light of bug lamps over our torches or candles, partly because we feared fire and partly because we did not need such strong illumination after our eyesight adjusted to the dark. Sora, on the other hand, whose eyes were even worse than mine, had all three of our torches lit by the time I got to our dwelling.

"Is the house on fire?" I asked loudly while rubbing the dirt from my feet and blinking my eyes. The torches were like suns blazing even through the many hanging herbs drying around our home.

"Oh hush, Agi, and come eat your dinner in peace."

Sora was already at the table drinking from a clay bowl filled with HoFe soup. This is a cold soup much like your planet's ceviche, in which raw fish "cooks" in acidic fruit juice along with vegetables and herbs. Her face, a premature gray, was jolly from the teasing, and as she placed her bowl back on the table, she laughed again.

"You wouldn't be laughing if you'd spent the day gathering palm leaves," I grumbled as I took my place at the second stool. "Look at these paws." I held them up to show off the wounds, red lines that crossed the pads and disappeared into the fur.

"Yes, I heard about our new visitors." Likely our son had come around, which explained the fresh fish I'd had no time to catch. Then again, as one of our people's only healers, Sora always had many gossipers eager to fill her in on the newest blather. "You're not the only one working overtime. General Fah also assigned me two new assistants to gather herbs for healing potions. He guesses we will need them by the bucketful once the Adalaffians leave their ship. Perhaps he senses peace on the horizon?"

"Only time will tell. Did he gift us a second dwelling to hold all of those herbs?" I asked. To make my point, I batted at a vine, dried and gray, that hung two inches from the top of my head. Through the small forest hung upside-down in our room, I could barely see our bed or the wooden divider between where we sat and the small space designated for the chamber pot and the pulley that lowered it to the ground.

"Oh, stop your complaining. How many times have you disturbed a nest and gotten an arm full of stingers?" she asked as she grabbed the end of the vine, crushed it in her paw, and rubbed the dry flakes into my wounds. "How many times have you forgotten not to step in the black ivy and come home itching your fur off? How many times—"

"Alright, alright, you've made your point. I'm your best customer." The wound began to burn, so I pulled my paw away and licked at it some more. Then I took a long slurp of soup and licked the lemony aftertaste from my lips. Delicious. "All I'm saying is that a storeroom wouldn't be a bad idea."

"And who will build it?" Sora asked, her eyebrows rising. "You can barely get up the ramp these days."

I straightened my shoulders. "I will remind you that I am a soldier in General Fah's army, and that such a position demands respect!"

"You are General Fah's cousin, Agi." She shook her head. "Any other soldier your age would have long been removed from service."

I huffed and returned to my soup. She was right, of course she was right, and yet back then I would never have admitted it. As long as I could still do the training maneuvers—albeit slower than the rest of my unit—I would show up every morning for service until someone stopped me.

"Tell me about what happened on the field," she said. She probably knew I was itching to tell my story.

"I'm too old to remember," I groused.

"Please?"

"Fine." I finished my soup in two long slurps and sat back with my hands on my belly. "But not a single interruption!"

####

My back woke me the next morning, the ache now all the way up to my shoulders and throbbing. "Uhhh," I moaned as I slowly used my hands in a crab crawl to raise myself up from the net stretched from one wall to the other. Then I scooted across on my bottom until I could throw my aching body off the net to the floor.

"I feel like that brown leaf cream would do wonders for me…" I mumbled, hoping to wake Sora, but she stirred behind me and resettled in a curled ball under the covers. "Fine. I'll find a cure myself."

Sora kept her medicines in glass vials from the humans. Before their arrival, Sora had carried the herbs loose in a bag, and whenever she was called to a sickbed, she would have to combine or even cook the poultice on demand. Now that she had the vials—and assistants to help her—she made large batches in advance, including a soothing cream for my arthritis. But which one was mine? I stared at the shelves, and the creams organized by color from pink to neon green. Mine would be in the browns, I knew, with flecks of black seeds. I tentatively lifted a vial and opened the stopper to sniff.

Earthy. Hint of sour garlic; hint of berry sweetness. Yes, that was mine, I was sure of it. After finding a piece of natural sponge in one of the jars on the counter, I drenched the applicator in cream and lifted the sponge as far behind me as I could.

"Agi, no!" Sora had come up behind me, and now she hit the sponge out of my hand so that it left a print on the far wall. "How many times—" she huffed as she batted at my now empty hands, "—have I told you not to play healer?"

"I think I know my own medicine," I said.

"Oh, really?" She snatched the vial up from the counter and waved it in front of my face. "Because this is a sleeping potion. You didn't notice the zeezee stingers floating in there?"

Zeezee stingers. Not seeds.

My mistake.

"It's no fault of mine that you hide my treatment," I grumbled.

"Hide it?" She pointed at a vial on the center table with my name written on the side. "Is that what you call hiding it?"

What could I say to that?

Once Sora soothed my back and wrapped up some cheese and bread for my breakfast, I descended the ramp at a slow amble. Most of the HoFe would sleep until noon, but those of us in the official army would be summoned for drills at 10:00 A.M. sharp by a special beating of two spears against a hollow stump. I owned no clock, but judging by the sun, the time was between 8:00 and 9:00 A.M. I had time to kill, and no one to talk to.

Not really thinking too much, I wandered out of our camp and toward the empty field where our almost-battle had occurred the day before. As I drew closer to the edge of the forest, I heard voices talking quietly and, underneath the murmur, some singing. Curious, I peered through the last row of trees at the busy Adalaffians, who were hard at work weaving the palm leaves around the rods we had gathered the day before. They sat in three circles around three piles of divided bounty, and I noted, again, how indistinct they all were from each other. Every Adalaffian even moved in a kind of unison, so that their hands were like fish darting between hiding spots as they swept the leaves over, under, over to the time of the music. I thought of ants carrying pieces of a dead carcass back in a line, or of bees working on a hive.

A twig broke nearby. My claws snapped out, and I raised my paws instinctively toward the sound of the attacker. It was Sig, recognizable by the tattoos on their chest and lack of hair.

"You shouldn't be in here alone," I scolded. Yes, you heard right, simple Agi spoke to the leader of the Adalaffians like they were a naughty child.

"You're correct." Sig shrugged. "I guess after years of being stuck on boats, and then a spaceship, I just needed to walk a bit."

"Well, walk on the hofellium field," I said, but my voice tempered now. "Your people would hate to lose their leader now, when they need you most."

"I'm no leader." Sig looked through the trees at the Adalaffians. "My father was a leader. The elders before him were leaders. I'm just in charge because I don't trust anyone else."

"After what I've seen," I said, thinking of the first arrival of The Santa Clara, "you might be right not to."

Sig asked me my name, and I told them. Then we watched the weaving for a few minutes in silence. It had a calming effect, those upward and downward movements, and my breathing slowed to a peaceful tempo. My tail came to rest against the back of my legs. Yet when I looked back at Sig, their hands balled and their shoulders tense, they seemed angry.

"I hate weaving," they said when they caught me staring.

"Really? But I thought your people—"

"Necessity." Their hands relaxed, but their shoulders stayed up. "And the fact that these generations know nothing of our previous life on Laffa. My mother was an engineer; my father was a member of the space program."

"Is that why he...?"

Sig crossed their arms and rubbed their tattoos. "I don't know if it's delusions of grandeur from his time with the humans, or plain old meanness, or some secret reason that he decided not to share on the weeks-long trip to get here—and I don't really care."

I looked at the Adalaffian ship where Tamalin was prisoner.

"You know," I mused, "when my son was a small child, he went through a phase where he was moody and withdrawn. One day, he waited until we left to gather berries and then took control of our home. Whenever we tried to climb the ramp, he pelted Sora's precious potions down at us, including a mix that burned my spouse so badly she had to be healed by one of her assistants. Even then, as she screamed on the ground, my son would not stop throwing the vials."

"How did you get him to stop?" Sig asked. His shoulders had finally leveled.

"I didn't." I ripped off a leaf from a nearby palm, checked it for insects, threw it out onto the field, and ripped off another. As our saying goes, *Lazy hands make a lazy head.*

Alright, fine, I'll admit it. I was embarrassed about my role in the story, and I regretted mentioning it in the first place.

"Eventually, he ran out of potions, and pots, and even chairs," I said, a small pile growing at my feet. "When I got up to the house, I tied him up to one of the posts and left him there until Sora was healed enough to return and give him a calming medication." My ripping increased in speed. "Years later, my son told me that the reason he did all of that was because he did not want to be a soldier in General Fah's army—that he was a pacifist, to use a human word—and that he was scared that we would be disappointed in his decision."

Sig imitated my motion and added their own palm leaf to the pile. "You seem to be trying to teach me a lesson, Agi, but I'm not sure what it is. I suspect that these stories and metaphors work better on your species than mine. Speak your mind plainly."

"I apologize," I said, pulling off an ant from a leaf and flicking it away from us. "What I meant to say is: Why don't you just ask him?"

Sig did not seem offended by my words, and in fact, they appeared to muse on them as we parted ways. I admired that trait about them, and though they might not have seen themselves as a leader, I already suspected they would play a continued role in the relations between our two peoples.

I went back home to complete my morning drills, where our stretches finally loosened the stiffness of my aching back just in time for the pushups to make new aches in my shoulders. General Fah did not make things easy on us, even after the previous day's gathering and the coming afternoon repetition, and even the young soldiers left the drills groaning and rubbing their sore thighs.

During that time, Sig apparently returned to *The Santa Clara* to talk to their father.

Of course, you already know what they discovered.

Still, for the record: An hour after drills, two Adalaffians came running through the forest into our central clearing, having found it again with the help of the two HoFe guards assigned to the edge of the woods. The Adalaffians were out of breath, having never run long distances in their lives, and they had to rest before they could speak again. Their skin was an even deeper green then normal.

"Tamalin," one of them got out.

"HoFe," gasped the other.

"What about HoFe?" General Fah demanded.

One of the Adalaffians took a deep inhalation and then rushed in one long breath: "Sig just found out that Tamalin never planned to move our people to HoFe but just wanted to use this planet as a rest stop where we could manufacture weapons using the hofellium and dig up some fuel and then he was going to get back on the ship and use *The Santa Clara* to attack Earth and win a piece of the planet for the Adalaffians."

The Adalaffian might have said more, but then they passed out with a disturbing thump. A minute later their breathing returned to normal, and their skin paled to a less alarming green. "Go get a smelling salt from Sora," I ordered one of the other soldiers nearby. Technically I should have gone, but I wasn't about to miss what happened next. The soldier gave me a bewildered look, but then she scampered off.

"What are they talking about?" General Fah said to the other Adalaffian. "Why would Tamalin try to take our planet if he did not intend to stay here?"

"Because," the second Adalaffian huffed, "the humans had mapped the global warming of your planet."

"Our what?" I butted in.

"Your…" They waved their hands at the ground and then collapsed them. "Your planet's atmosphere. It's thinning. Soon—very soon—this planet will be inhospitable to any lifeforms."

We all stared at the Adalaffian blankly, even General Fah. None of us had given any thought to our atmosphere or were even quite sure what the word meant. Sure, the weather had been a bit hot lately, but HoFe was always hot.

"How else can I say it?" the Adalaffian gasped. "How about this: In fifty years, you'll all be dead!"

The second Adalaffian collapsed, but nobody even noticed.

####

In a way, you might say I, Agi the Elder, saved the HoFe from extinction.

If I had not asked General Sig to speak to their father, they might never have found out about the atmosphere. They might never have left our planet, and they might never have travelled across the universe to your Earth to seek vengeance. The whole course of our shared histories would have been altered—or even ended.

What was that?

Tamalin would have eventually told somebody?

Well, I supposed you're right.

But that version doesn't make for nearly as good of a story, does it?

Goodness, we're out of time for today. Please come to our next meeting prepared to discuss the supplemental reading "HoFe Battle Tactics"; if I'm feeling accommodating, we'll even discuss a HoFeLaffian law or two.

ARTICLE TWENTY-ONE

Doctor Janamin's Report

Curator's Note: Doctor Janamin was the Council's first official advisor on all matters pertaining to the human body. As is evidenced in this report, the doctor often claimed to speak for the entire HoFeLaffian medical community, which eventually led to the creation of a counter-collective, accurately called The HoFeLaffian Society of Medical Professionals Advocating for the Human Race, or HSMPAHR, and then a counter-counter-collective, led by none other than Doctor Janamin, called The HoFeLaffian Society for the Acknowledgement of the Lesser Species. Both HSMPAHR and HSALS were eventually deemed insurgent organizations and disbanded.

Humans.

As Tamalin said, they are a strange race.

Just their consumption alone leaves questions. Sugar, which leads to higher blood pressure, weight gain, and diabetes. Fat, which leads to heart attack and stroke. Alcohol, which they cannot tolerate nearly as well as the Adalaffians and which leads them to deadly delusions of grandeur. Tobacco, the first leading, preventable cause of death.

In every act of their daily lives, they will risk their own lives and the lives of others with a casualness that still surprises.

No wonder their life span is so short.

After the HoFeLaffa took control of Earth, these destructive habits increased exponentially. It seems that, unlike the life-worshipping Adalaffa and the honorable fighters of the HoFe, humans value their freedom most of all. Rule from foreign races was like trapping them in a car trunk and throwing the key in the river. Ironic, considering that before the HoFeLaffa elders took over for Congress, HealthCorp had long been in charge of both the major and minor aspects of every citizen's life, from what vitamins they chewed every morning to what they heard on the news every night—but these levels of critical thought do not seem to occur often in the human brain, overpowered, as they are, by the amygdala.

They have also taken up new traditions.

For example, the bands of wild youth who roam the streets looking for lone HoFeLaffians. These children are like the rabid dogs that once lived in alleys, vicious and unrelenting. Just this year, they began accompanying their gruesome stabbings of HoFeLaffians with the words "Go home" painted on the building walls in green, blue, and orange blood. They also collected the extra blood in vials and distributed the colorful ampoules amongst themselves, so as to recognize other gang members on the streets, though the modern fashion trend these containers inspired has made it impossible to actually use them as a method of arrest.

For example, the refusal to work.

Not just for HoFeLaffian bosses, but for any company that hires HoFeLaffian employees—effectively every company, since the equality quota is now law. These humans sit at home and resent the loss of their positions, even as essential business after essential business folds.

Again, that amygdala, so small and yet so powerful, seems to run their whole limbic system.

There are other mysteries about this strange race. For example, their religions, which are full of contradictions—that one might see God's face, and yet that such a vision is impossible; that one might take an eye for an eye, and yet turn the other cheek.

That the end is at hand—always and never.

Such illogicalities do not bother the humans; in fact, they seem to use them as justifications for a variety of equally contradictory beliefs and actions. Even in their distaste for their new rulers, they seem divided, with a strange subset of humans completely embracing the lifestyles of the HoFeLaffa in strange and cultish communities called "Dens." These "Dens" practice amplified versions of the traditional HoFe and Laffian traditions, such as basket weaving, morning training, metal forging, and consuming unhealthy amounts of polluted seaweed.

For example, their gender divisions.

The humans seem to have an innate desire to categorize. Based on studies of this species, medical diagnoses have determined that, though there may be minor improvements in their behavior over generations, this constant cataloging and hierarchical thinking, mixed with a violent nature, will eventually lead the humans to attack.

Thus, it is the agreement of the HoFeLaffa medical community that those not of Earth must either seize this planet for themselves or find an alternate living place for our future generations.

In summary: there can be no peace.

ARTICLE TWENTY-TWO

From *Elder Tales: HoFeLaffian Lessons for Human Children*

There once was an elder named Aduna the Red. On the day of her birth, Aduna dropped from her mother as red and round as a hofellium nugget. "Tragic," her birth guide exclaimed as she rubbed a towel over Aduna's fur. "This one is destined for a bad end." Her mother changed her name from *child of laughter* to "Aduna," which means *child of stone*.

As Aduna grew up, she developed a special affinity for her namesake. She walked miles a day through the ghost lands, and then, when she figured out how to make a shovel with a stick, buried her legs in the dusty fields. With the hofellium nuggets, she drew patterns around herself, like mandalas in their geometrical design, and these she left for as long as the wind withheld its dust. If the patterns meant anything to Aduna, she did not explain it to her mother or the people who came to find her when the sun set. Looking over the ghost lands of the empty hofellium fields back then was like looking at the landscape of some other alien planet.

"Oh, Aduna," her mother always said. "Don't you know you can't hide from a great destiny?"

"I'm right where I'm meant to be," said Aduna.

After her mother died, Aduna set up a tent deep in the ghost lands and never left. The people brought her fruit and fish and medicine when she was ill, believing, as our people often do with anomalies, that she was some kind of oracle. Her fur never grayed, but only deepened in its red color and thickened until you could barely see her two red eyes in their deep-set sockets. Those who brought offerings gave reports: Aduna had surrounded her tent with ten hofellium circles; Aduna had managed a small garden in the unforgiving earth; Aduna ate the hofellium flakes with her breakfast; Aduna had made claims of a greater purpose, one she would unfortunately not be able to fulfill.

"What purpose?" the people asked, but she wouldn't say.

On her deathbed, Aduna's great-niece stayed by her side, spooning her HoFe soup and singing the old death song until her voice grew hoarse. When it finally gave out completely, the niece sat down on the only chair in the tent and put her hands on Aduna's tail.

"I have not fulfilled my purpose," Aduna whispered hoarsely.

The niece could not reply.

"I was to be the protector of the Hofellium," Aduna continued. She could finally speak about her heavy burden now that it had slipped from her shoulders—or maybe she had finally gone mad. "You must call yourself Aduna and take up my post. When the new arrivals come, you must greet them, and then you must find a method of sending them away."

Ironically, when the humans landed on HoFe, Aduna the Second was the one to walk them through the forest to meet the General.

None of this is important, of course.

What matters is that we now know, from Aduna's tale and then later human trials, is that too much hofellium consumption can turn an individual as red as a nugget. It can also put them into toxic shock, as it likely did Aduna. So be careful, children of Earth, and never use hofellium for recreational purposes.

####
####

WARNING: IF YOU ACCIDENTALLY SWALLOW HOFELLIUM, PLEASE CALL (800) 222-1222.

ARTICLE TWENTY-THREE

JoJo's Deposition

December 12, 2159

My full name is Jomalin Laffa Fah Junior, but my friends call me JoJo. I am a human, and though I was raised with a genderqueer identity, I now identify as a man. Please refer to me with the pronoun "he."

I was born in a Den off the coast of what was once California, where my parents, former Vice Presidents for HealthCorp, had recently given up their materialistic lifestyle after their "wakeup" on Arrival Day and donated their beachside mansion to the cause. By the time I was born—a water birth, of course, though that was actually a human ritual—there were twenty-five followers of the HoFeLaffa living in huts in our backyard.

The huts were made of woven materials. Every time it rained, everyone had to gather in the living room and wait out the storm while streams of water inundated the huts. During the worst storms, our homes were flattened.

This did not seem to bother anyone but me.

Things could be worse, the followers were fond of saying. *At least we're safe on dry land.* They said the same about the days when local seaweed harvesting restrictions changed from 10 pounds a day to five pounds a day—probably because of our Den—and the times when Joe burned his hand so badly trying to forge a HoFellian blade that he had to be sent to the emergency room.

All this, while the true HoFeLaffians bought penthouses in the metropolis.

Thinking back to those days, I can still smell salt and hear waves. My hands sweat in imitation of the slime of the green algae. My stomach aches, empty from any sustenance but bread and seaweed gruel.

Yet these are memories tainted by my adulthood.

The truth is that at the time, I loved living in our Den. What child does not idolize spending their days on the beach chasing crabs and gathering litter to use as hanging decorations in the huts? I was not alone, either; I had friends, two of them, also named after great Laffian elders but nicknamed Prawn and Catfish, and the three of us prowled the shoreline day and night like beach mice.

Children of the Den began HoFe fight training at ten years old—roughly the equivalent to the HoFe's twenty-year start point, considering their lengthy lifespan. That morning, Prawn and Catfish ran through our hut naked and screaming in wild anticipation: "We are warriors!" They looked similar to me, all flat-chested nakedness and bare legs interrupted only by the Den's woven fabric shorts, but distinct in that Prawn was a scrawny red-head and Catfish had a mouth that stretched almost all the way across their face.

I use the pronoun "their" here in the way that the Laffians do, but of course, we had distinct sexual traits where the Laffian children had none. Following traditional assignments of sexes, Prawn was a biological boy, and Catfish was a biological girl. Yet we did not know any of this—not until our teen years, when things suddenly happened to our bodies the way the tectonic shifts happened on Adalaffa and we became aware of ourselves, and of the world. Then we discovered the human concepts of assigned sexes, and gender identities, and the emphasis on pronouns.

At the time, we were one pack.

I sprung from my mat and let out an excited yowl in the tradition of the HoFe battle cry. My fingers went up to my head in the imitation of ears, and I perked them up and waved my butt where a tail should have been. My parents, slender and muscular under their seaweed tunics from their gathering, patted my head in turn and told me, *We're so proud of you.* My father had a beard then, wild like a beach cabbage, and my mother's long hair was dyed a plain, Laffian brown.

I scarfed down my gruel and then followed Prawn and Catfish through the curtain to the open part of the yard, where Master Fah the Second—born Donny Brown, legendary former Jiu Jitsu instructor, but again, I did not know that at the time—waited with our breastplates and wooden knives. The real armor, composed of scraps of rare hofellium mixed with iron and leather, was reserved for fully trained soldiers, so our breastplates were only leather scraps sewn together like patchwork quilts and our swords were wood shaved into shape by Donny. The leather quilt was heavy and hot on my chest; the sword was awkward and too short for a child my size.

Years later, this memory would be tainted by the new knowledge that the HoFe did not even fight with swords at all, but rather spears. By then, however, I would already know that almost nothing we practiced in our Den was actually accurate.

Maybe accuracy wasn't the point.

"Welcome, warriors," Donny said as he bowed and then handed us each a set of armor. He was decked out in the Den's best uniform—full hofellium breastplate purchased with the last of my parents' savings and a rare katana sword with a curved blade—and had his head and face covered by an iron helmet. His shaggy beard had been trimmed for this occasion, and his shorts were newly woven. "You are my first new recruits, so the responsibility of proving the worth of our Den falls to you."

We held our shoulders higher.

Donny showed us a few of the traditional HoFe moves, and we imitated them, from crouching in an attack stance to pouncing with our swords raised. These feline motions felt awkward to our very human bodies, which could not spring forward or backward with any kind of grace. Prawn fell on their backside while trying to dodge Donny's blow. Catfish dropped their sword every few minutes and broke the HoFe façade with the use of a Laffian curse invented after the arrival of *The Santa Clara: Damalaffa*, which roughly translates to *Damn your life*. I managed to stay upright, but my legs burned from the strain of all of the squatting and seizing.

We should have had low expectations for ourselves—after all, the adults who had been participating in Donny's morning drills looked only slightly less awkward during their own trainings—but we had assumed that as the first Den Born, we would be special.

After crouching and pouncing, we learned several other sword thrusts and combinations. My favorite was called The Branaynay, when the warrior leaps forward with both feet like a frog and then sticks their sword straight into their opponent's chest. The leather did little to stop the impact of the swords, and soon, all three of us had large blue bruises like lakes across the landscapes of our chests and backs.

"Enough," Donny finally called out, and we collapsed in the grass like a pile of playful kittens. "You have made our Den proud."

The police, both human and HoFeLaffian, were always trying to shut down our Den. Frequently, they were assisted by the neighbors, who constantly reported our strange behaviors. The human cops were mean—

the rest of our species saw the Den-dwellers as traitors—and the HoFeLaffian cops were condescending, as were the HoFeLaffian EMTs called the time my mom accidentally poisoned my dad with an imitation HoFe potion, as were the HoFeLaffian firefighters who put out the forge fires more times than I can remember, and the HoFeLaffian weaving instructor who we hired to explain why our seaweed huts kept leaking.

Or maybe they were just confused as to why a bunch of privileged humans who had never suffered the threat of killer seaweed or endured a year-long space voyage to escape planet-wide destruction insisted on living that way.

When I was fifteen, my parents told me that we were going to have a special visit from a HoFeLaffian named Jaydin, who had been a child himself during the Laffian voyage from Adalaffa to HoFe. He had been hired by the Den elders who met biannually to share his story and advise us on best practices, and we were his third stop.

On the day of his arrival, our whole Den gathered on the front lawn to greet him. While we waited, passersby in their cars honked at us; one waved his middle finger and shouted "Long Laffa, idiots!" I felt self-conscious in a way I wasn't used to. Sure, people tanning on the beach stared as we collected seaweed from piles on the sand or ran through our drills, but tuning them out was a skill I'd had years to develop.

Maybe I felt self-conscious because I was about to meet a *real* HoFeLaffian—and if he was real, then what was I?

Finally, Jaydin arrived in a black car with tinted windows—the kind of car I imagined my parents owned before they sold all of their belongings—and after him climbed out two additional Laffians, who turned out to be his spouse, Camilin, and their child, Sashan. All three had green skin, green eyes, and brown hair, but their styles—Jaydin in a suit, Camilin in a sheath dress and heels, and Sashan in a white jumper that did not mark them as a specific gender—made them distinct. From what I had overheard from conversations on the beach, the Adalaffians were now the world's largest consumers of luxury clothing, and these three were no exception.

"Long laffa," my father called out.

"Long laffa," the three Laffians echoed.

They followed us through the house. The rooms were empty of their original furniture, and the white walls had long ago accumulated dust and dirt. Each room had a new purpose: for example, the living room was for weapons storage, the dining room was for weaving supplies, and the kitchen was for distilling gin. Sandy streaks made a carpet for our bare feet as we filed down the hallway and out the back door to the deck, where we gathered at night for our HoFe-style bonfires and story tellings. From the raised platform, Jaydin surveyed the huts below.

"I'll speak to your Den founders," he said finally. "The rest of you, please go about your traditional days; I will come question you individually later on."

The crowd dispersed, but I stayed with my parents so as not to miss a single minute with the HoFeLaffians. My parents offered Jaydin's family mats around the blackened fire pit, which they took after dusting off the fabric first.

"How many are you?" Jaydin asked once we settled.

"We currently have thirty-five residents," said my mom. "We capped the original group at twenty-five, but of course…" She waved a hand to me, a Den-born.

"Of course. And your primary activities are?"

"Seaweed collection, weaving, and military training," answered my dad. "We have several amateur storytellers and one healer, who is assisted by my wife, a level three potion mixer."

Jaydin removed a cell phone from his pocket and typed. I had seen these devices frequently on the beach, but never so close. They seemed… The feeling is hard to explain. Absorbing, yes, but also mildly threatening.

"And your financial situation?" Jaydin asked.

"Moderate, for a Den," said my father. "My wife and I own the house and land, and we have a tax exemption due to our religious status. To pay for our additional bills, like hospital stays and basic house mainte-nance, the group sells our extra seaweed gin. We also have an online store for some of our armor, which, as you know, has become quite popular in the metropolis as wall décor."

Most of this was new information for me. An online store? Who updated it, and on what technology? My parents seemed like strangers, and even their voices had changed tones—all business. I also noticed new things about them then, like the way my mother's hair had grown in gray at the roots and my father's beard had thinned. Their seaweed tunics needed mending, and the bottoms of their bare feet were browned and calloused from so much beach walking. Compared to our sophisticated visitors, they seemed... well, truthfully, they seemed out of their minds.

"Very good." Jaydin jotted down a few more notes. "Now, if you'll excuse me, I'll go walk around the Den and inspect daily operations for myself. You'll receive my official report in three days."

He left us. My parents offered Camilin some gin, and soon they, too, had disappeared. Sashan and I stared at each other over the pit.

"Your family's pretty weird," they said.

"In what way?" The words sounded defensive, though I had meant to appear nonchalant.

"Uh." Their eyes roamed the yard. "All ways."

This conversation was not going well. I could tell I was blushing because I felt like I had sunburn even though my skin had long lost the ability to brown further.

"Well, your family's pretty weird too," I fired back. "I mean, what kind of HoFeLaffians dress like human dolls and make money off of hardworking Den-dwellers who just want get close to nature and enjoy their lives?"

Sashan opened their mouth and closed it. Then they looked down at the hem of their top leg and scratched at an invisible spot. I noticed they had a tattoo on their arm: the name Raya, written in a Laffian seaweed script.

"Sorry." I took a deep breath, like Donny had taught us to do before firing a weapon, and then said something I had not even known I felt: "It's bad enough the whole world thinks we're a joke."

"You are a joke," said Sashan in a kinder voice, "but I guess I sort of get the appeal. Living in the metropolis can be super stressful, and we never have time to just breathe. Gathering seaweed and weaving and stuff sounds nice. Like a vacation."

"It is pretty idyllic," I said. "But…"

"But?"

Before I could voice any other secret thoughts, my parents came back with Camilin and a tray filled with mugs of gin. Sashan and I got gin too—underage drinking was another benefit of a religious exemption—and we sat quietly and listened to our parents talk until Jaydin returned.

"You'll be hearing from me soon," he said, finally putting his cell phone in his pocket. "Don't worry, we can see ourselves out."

####

The next time I met Sashan was in a college classroom.

I did not recognize them at first. Telling one Laffian from another was more a matter of their style than your memory, and the Laffian sitting two rows in from of me in "History of the HoFeLaffians" wore a plain white t-shirt and black skinny jeans. During notetaking, I spotted a black Raya tattoo in seaweed script, but again, that was as common as braids or the rare individual with blue skin.

Professor Agi was in the middle of telling us about the Adalaffian arrival on HoFe, an event that he had lived through as a "younger old man." I could not picture him as anything but hunched over his cane, with gray fur and a tail that only switched downward against the linoleum.

"Yes, Sashan?" he asked when the Laffian raised their hand.

Sashan. Yes, I definitely knew that name.

"My aunt Bina says that if Tamalin had not been shot, the Adalaffians would have been slaughtered by the HoFe before they even made it to the forest line. Do you agree with that statement?"

Yes, I definitely knew that challenging tone.

Professor Agi gave them a thin-lined smile. "Off the record? They wouldn't have made it halfway across the field."

The class murmured.

"Even with an equal number of human guns?" Sashan pressed.

The rest of us exchanged *Can you believe this?* glances. Arguing with a professor always made everyone uncomfortable; then again, if they were anything like me, they were also curious to hear the answer.

"Let me tell you a little story," said Professor Agi. He leaned back against his desk and leaned his cane against the side. "There once were two fraternal twins: Gafifi and Rafifi. As teens, they fell in love with the same woman, and when they were of age, they decided to have a duel for her hand. Each twin selected one weapon for the fight; Gafifi selected a HoFe spear, and Rafifi selected a human gun. I should add that rather than putting our backs together and walking apart, a HoFe duel requires that both parties hide behind trees roughly twenty feet apart and then spring out at the sound of a special drum. Anyway, the morning came, and the twins hid behind their trees. The drum sounded. Both leapt out, and the one with the gun, Rafifi, fired an initial bullet. Do you know what happened then?"

No one spoke.

Professor Agi chuckled. "Nothing! As it turned out, Rafifi had forgotten to actually load his gun that morning! He bent down to find his pouch of bullets, and bam, Gafifi's spear went straight into the right side of his chest."

"I'm not sure what the point of this story—" Sashan began.

"The point, my fellow HoFeLaffian, is that a gun only shoots the bullets. It's the warrior behind the gun who aims the weapon—or, in this case, the spear. In the story, Gafifi aims for his brother's right side in order to seriously wound him but not kill him because HoFe hearts, like the humans', are on the left side. He gets the girl, keeps his brother alive, and lives happily ever after."

"So you're saying that the HoFe had skills that—" Sashan pressed again.

In the time it took me to blink, Professor Agi kicked his cane up in the air, pressed some kind of lever on the side, and launched it. The cane—or what had once been a cane but was now a spear with two protruding blades—stuck into the exact center of the poster of Earth hanging on the wall behind us with a sharp *thwap*.

"Any other questions?" Professor Agi asked.

"You've answered mine, thank you," said an unfazed Sashan.

"Good." Professor Agi stroked his chin fur. "Now, can anyone tell me what I was going to discuss today?"

After class, I caught up with Sashan in the hallway. I tugged on the smooth leather strap of their designer messenger bag, and when they turned and gave me a haughty stare, I said quickly, "My name is JoJo. We met at my parents' Den a few years ago?"

Sashan looked me up and down. I felt more conscious than normal of my NYU sweatshirt, unbrushed hair, and hippie sandals. Before I had moved across the country, I had imagined myself as transforming into a real metropolis man upon my arrival, but as I mentioned earlier, leaving the Den had given me a new perspective on that idyllic, sunbaked seaweed life. During my first semester, I had found myself dressing like an old-school surfer, weaving as a form of stress relief, and seeking out buying bottles of seaweed gin I drank right before bed so that the smell lingered into my sleep.

Basically, I missed home.

Sashan's look softened slightly. "JoJo. Yes, I actually do remember you. The fact that you're wearing a shirt now must have thrown me off."

I blushed. "Back home going bare-chested all the time was normal—"

They put up a hand to stop me. "Trust me, I know. My father advised Dens for a living, remember? I must have met five hundred shirtless humans during the last few years—though I don't remember them as well as I do you."

I wasn't sure what to say to that, so I didn't say anything. Luckily. Sashan had enough confidence for both of us.

"Want to come over to my place for a drink?" they asked.

That was how I found myself in a sky rise on the Upper East Side drinking a cup of seaweed gin while drones flew by like terns diving for schooling fish. The city looked different from that view, and for the first time in months, I felt less like plankton sucked in by a whale and more like…well, a slightly bigger aquatic organism. I took another sip and then asked how they had gotten out of the normal student-housing requirement.

Apparently, Sashan's dad now did more than advise Dens; he also owned his own luxury fashion line.

"When I have spare time, I design for them," said Sashan casually as they propped their black loafers up on the balcony railing. I noticed the S stamped in the leather and wondered if it stood for Sashan. "By the way, did your parents let you leave the Den, or did you run away?"

"A little bit of both?"

The truth was that I had found the secret computer from which my parents had been running their online businesses and worked on my application during the middle of the night. My admissions essay, "Den Life," had taken me over two months to write. Though I'd kept the process a secret, on the day the acceptance email came through, I had told my parents the truth. They were disappointed, but they understood. *You'll come back,* my dad had said confidently. *There's less out there than you think.*

Turns out, he was right.

After our drinks, Sashan invited me to stay for dinner. They knew a little Italian eatery that delivered, and with three simple taps to their phone, ordered us a meal. Fifteen minutes after that—in the time it took me to tell a story about the time the whole Den got measles and forgot all about the food—a quadcopter buzzed up to the railing and toward us like a persistent horsefly. Unfortunately, my HoFe warrior instincts kicked in, and I delivered the drone a deadly blow to the far right rotor with my closest hand— the one holding my empty glass.

The glass almost flew over the side of the balcony, but luckily, it bounced off the railing first before tumbling back toward me and then breaking. At the same time, the quadcopter spun and then crashed down with a dramatic clack and scrape. The food bag came loose, slid across the floor, and hit the far wall, where grilled octopus spilled out of one of the containers in a convincing display of revived life.

Slowly, I turned toward Sashan.

They were laughing at me, and not with any attempt to hide it.

"Sorry... I guess I... I've never ordered..." I looked back at the defeated drone, and at the camera eye facing my direction. "This is really embarrassing."

"It really is," agreed Sashan.

"Should we call the restaurant, or...?"

Sashan went over to the drone and flipped it. They typed a few numbers on their phone and then announced, "Now it's our broken drone."

"Oh. Thanks. I'll pay you back as soon as—"

"No need."

"But I feel terrible—"

Sashan held up their other hand to cut me off. "Honestly? You probably can't pay me back. I didn't check the price, but the ones we use to deliver cost around two thousand dollars. Don't worry about it."

Two thousand dollars? I wondered how much seaweed gin my

parents would have to sell to send me that much money. No, I couldn't tell them; I would need to get a job. But how could I get a job when I had no marketable skills yet?

"Is there anything else I can do to make it up to you?" I asked as Sashan bent down and retrieved two additional takeout containers, these ones miraculously undamaged by their fall.

"Actually, yes." Sashan handed me the containers, which were still warm on the bottom. "Buy yourself a new shirt and a pair of real shoes."

####

The containers turned out to be mushroom ravioli and broccolini with anchovies and garlic. The smell of fish mixed with vegetables made me think of home and the many times Prawn, Catfish, and I had gone out to the dock to catch our dinner, and how they were probably there now, rods in hand, silently waiting for a tug on their lines.

"Thinking of home?" asked Sashan.

I nodded. "As a teen, all I wanted to do was get away from there. Yet now that I succeeded, I miss it."

"Makes sense." They poured more gin into the plastic cup they had dug up from the back of their pantry. Hopefully, this one was indestructible. "Want to know a HoFeLaffian secret?"

"Sure."

They leaned back against their white linen chair and rested their gin glass against their chest. "We have that feeling all the time."

"What do you mean?"

"We even have a word for it: *Dualaffa*, 'the feeling of living a dual life.' According to psychologists, the offspring of Laffians have it worst of all because we are three times removed from our home planet: Adalaffa, then HoFe, then Earth. From what I've read, there was apparently some vitamin on Laffa that does not exist anywhere else in the galaxy, and the deficiency turns *Dualaffa* into both a physical and an emotional response. I suppose it's a lot like the humans whose depression worsens in winter."

"That sounds terrible."

Sashan shrugged. "It's a part of us. Friends I know who have mated have said it gets better—something about the accompanying hormonal changes, I guess. I wouldn't know."

I felt myself start to blush again at just the mention of the word mated. Ever since I'd seen Sashan again, I had wondered whether they had a spouse or, perhaps, had followed the human trend of casual hook-ups. From what I'd heard, the hook-ups also decided the gender of the Laffians in the way a formal coupling had, even though their contraception stopped them from conceiving. Sashan did not seem to have taken on one role or the other, and now I knew why.

"You can ask me," Sashan said.

I forced myself to take a deep breath. "Why haven't you...?"

"Never met the right mate." Sashan looked past me out the balcony door. "And besides, I don't really want to go through the changes that come with coupling. This version of me just feels like... well, like me."

"What about if you mated with a human? Would you still change?"

Had I just spoken those words out loud? I couldn't believe my boldness; and yet, I had been bold, for the first and only time in my life. There was something about Sashan that brought that man out in me, had done so since the very first time I'd seen them.

"I don't know," said Sashan, who stayed fully composed, as always. Then, they put their hand over mine.

####

You already know how this story ends—it is, after all, the reason I am here today. Sashan and I were the first HoFeLaffian and human to mate. Not only that, but it was our court case that made marriage between our species legal. As it turned out, mating with a human did not trigger the same hormonal responses in Laffians, and as a result, Sashan stayed Sashan.

As another result, Sashan's feeling of *Dualaffa* never went away.

They tried all kinds of cures, from HoFe potions to human anti-depressants. We spent winters at our lake house. We filled our social calendar with only Laffian friends. Nothing worked, and eventually, even our relationship—what Sashan had always referred to as their *reason for laffa*—began to change.

The last time I saw Sashan, we had just come back from visiting the Den. My parents had passed leadership of the group over to a younger couple, two Den-born who had new ideas for focusing on potion production and profit, and they now spent their days gathering seaweed along the coast and telling stories to the younger generation. Catfish had eventually gone to community college and then returned with a Clothing and Textiles major who knew more about weaving than anyone else, and the couple were planning on marrying in the HoFe tradition that summer. Prawn had disappeared one night and never come back. His parents had used Den funds to put out a bunch of television ads—ads that ironically they, as Den-dwellers, would never see—but so far, there had been no leads.

"It was nice, getting to see your parents," Sashan said while they unpacked their suitcase.

"Thanks for going." I put my arms around them. "Speaking of which, have you heard anything from your dad recently?"

Sashan stiffened. Jaydin had refused to acknowledge our union, and though, in the years since, he had eventually let me come to his house, we still saw him less than we saw my parents.

"*Dasalaffa*," Sashan cursed suddenly. *Damn his life.* "Why can't he accept us, the way your parents have?"

"Because for my parents, this is a dream come true," I said, letting go of their waist. "And remember, Jaydin's of a different generation."

"That's no excuse."

I could tell that Sashan was feeling low, so I let the subject drop.

We finished unpacking and then went out onto the patio for our nightly glass of gin. It was a nice night, but a bit cool; fall was on the horizon. Sashan was strangely quiet, and they drank a second, and then a third, glass.

"Are you okay?" I asked eventually. "I didn't mean to upset you by bringing up your dad."

"It's not that." Sashan lowered their nostril toward the gin and inhaled. "There was something about this trip to the Den... The smell of the ocean... I can't explain it. I stayed up all night listening to the waves. It felt like something inside of me—"

The doorbell rang.

"I'll get it," I said. "I think what's-her-name is coming by to get your signature on some new designs."

"Jen," Sashan said without looking at me. Their eyes were focused somewhere in the distance. "She's actually semi-competent, believe it or not. I guess fifth time's the charm."

"Sixth," I said.

"Sixth?"

I looked at Sashan pointedly. "Trust me, I know. I'm the one who had to fire all of her predecessors, remember?"

Sashan did not notice my look or tone of voice. I got up and went to the door, where I slipped from my silk slippers into my leather loafers and then padded across the apartment to the door. Sure enough, it was Jen, a small HoFelaffian with a brown nose instead of pink and claws that were always painted white. I wondered if the nose was real, or if she'd had the coloring professionally enhanced.

"Sorry to bother you," she started as soon as the door opened, "but I need Sashan's signature on these pants before tomorrow morning's design meeting."

"Sure. Just give me a minute, okay?"

I took the tablet from her paws and turned around.

The balcony was empty.

"Sashan?" I asked. Then I said their name again, louder.

No one answered.

No one ever asks me point blank if, knowing that Sashan would take their life, I would have made a different decision that day in class.

Still, I can tell that they want to ask, that the words are always on the tips of their tongues.

Would I have still stopped them in the hallway?

Would I have gone to their apartment?

Would I have purchased the new shirt and shoes I'd promised and then been pleased when they noticed?

No one ever asks—but I do, all of the time. I think about Sashan's life without me in it, and how much longer it would have lasted.

Dualaffa.

And yet I am a human, and therefore selfish.

I loved them.

What else can I say?

ARTICLE TWENTY-FOUR

Father Jeffrey's Story

People often ask me when I felt "called" to the priesthood, but the truth is, I always knew. My parents described me as a serious child, observant, always doodling in a sketchbook. Wild flowers, branches at odd angles, those trees with twisted trunks that look like a snake—these were the objects of my fascination. "Documenting," I called it. Documenting God's work. I imagined I saw him, like the back of someone turning around a corner, and that if I just looked hard enough, there he would be.

I was obedient at that age, but I also asked the hard questions. The whys. Growing up, my parents told everyone I would be a lawyer, so ready was I to build a case for or against a certain Bible verse. Mostly, I argued against the literal translation of a given text, instead embracing the beauty of a well-chosen metaphor—trumpets heard around the world, that kind of thing. And just because something was written down did not make it right. Perhaps this sounds like a strange disposition for a priest, but you'd be surprised. Most priests are scholars, are thinkers, and though they believe, they develop their faith over years of careful study and reflection.

As a result of a priest's strong conviction, many parishioners look to him or her for assurance—not just guidance, but certainty. My style of observation and calm argument has ruffled feathers at times, but, I believe, ultimately made my people more resolute in their faith.

Or, at least, it did.

After the chaos of Arrival Day, my congregation split into two. Half of them wanted to smite the Adalaffians; half of them wanted to worship them. Okay, I exaggerate—there were plenty of level-headed congregants—but they made themselves scarce as soon as the in-fighting began.

A year later, I did the same.

My retreat would be my house, I decided—not the parsonage, but the house where I had grown up, and where I had sat with my parents on their deathbeds not long before. I should have sold it, but I could not bring myself to let go of the garden where they had toiled on the weekends and drunk wine in their identical patio chairs. I told no one at the church where I was going.

Again, not exactly the actions of a model priest.

Looking back, I think I was going through a crisis of faith. I still believed in God, but beyond that, I could not be sure. So much death. So much fear. And that was just the human reaction, to say nothing of the

HoFeLaffians. All of this I pondered as I drove home, the landscaping changing quickly from city to suburb to farmland to forest. I reached the house around dinnertime.

A light in the window.

The sound of a record player—my father's, most likely. A family heirloom.

I got out and closed the door softly. My footsteps on the path were light—almost a tiptoe. I tried my key in the lock, but someone had changed the knob.

I rang the bell.

Someone approached through the wavy glass panes. A green face observed me. My hands shook in my pockets, so I took them out and clasped them. I wondered if I would have to fight for my home.

"May I help you?" asked the Laffian in the doorway.

Was that my high school track t-shirt? And my old gardening jeans?

"This is my house," I said, with more certainty than I felt.

The Laffian moved aside. "Come in."

I followed them, and they led me down the unaltered hallway where photos of me still adorned the walls. In the living room, my mother's crocheted blankets had been folded and put neatly into the baskets under the coffee table. The smell had changed slightly—something yeasty was in the air now, replacing the potpourri of my mother's bathroom—and there were a noticeable number of gin bottles on the counter.

"First, let me apologize," said the green Laffian now sitting comfortably in my father's armchair. On further inspection, they were slimmer than the average arrival, and their head was bald. Did Laffians normally have tattoos? "I assumed this house was unoccupied. I observed it for a year after Arrival Day before I moved in. I didn't want to stay in the city, but I had no money and nowhere else to go."

"This was my parents' house. They just died a few years ago."

"I'm sorry for your loss." They did look genuinely sorry, which I supposed made sense—loss of life and all that. "I will recite fifty laffas for them tonight, if that is acceptable."

"Of course."

How was I sitting in my parents' living room having a civil conversation with this alien squatter? Had I stepped into some kind of alternate universe when I left the parsonage—or perhaps out of one? I kept trying to work up the nerve to ask them to leave, but for some reason, I couldn't. Not because I was afraid, but because, in my t-shirt and jeans, this Laffian looked like they were exactly where they belonged.

"My name is Father Jeffrey," I said, holding out my hand.

"Sig," they said.

I tried to place the name. Sig... Sig... "I know that name. You can't be—”

“I’m not a general anymore,” Sig said. “I’m just a Laffian trying to survive.”

####

Arrival Day had apparently not gone as planned. The humans had been hostile, and the HoFeLaffians… Well, who could blame them? One of Sig’s siblings had been killed during the takeover of MediaCorp; one had been injured but survived to become the mother of an Earth-born Laffian. “HoFeLaffians,” Sig corrected themself. “I’m still getting used to that.”

“I mean, you are quite distinctly different, aren’t you?” I asked as I sat down on the bar stool at the island.

“Quite.” They poured me a generous glass of gin, which I accepted. “But on the journey here, we decided that those differences mattered less than our common goal. We needed a new home, and we needed…”

“Revenge?”

Sig tapped their glass. “I don’t like to think of what happened on Arrival Day as revenge. Justice, maybe, but even that feels inaccurate. We needed to make what you humans call a ‘big splash’—we needed to show you that we were here to stay. Mess that up, I told General Fah, and the humans would capture us and turn us into zoo animals. Arrival Day gave us a ‘seat at the table,’ to use another one of your expressions—at the head of the table.”

"Why do you sound so repentant, then?" I pressed.

Sig ran their hand over their bare head, where a little brown stubble had grown in since their last shave, and I wondered how old they were. No one, including the HoFe, seemed to know the Laffian life span, and the mystery gave them power—like gods.

"Because Bren is dead. And because making the right choice is not the same as making a good choice. I don't regret what happened, but yet, now that my people have survived and the burden of saving them has gone, I feel great sadness. Laffa was lost—and without respect for laffa, we might as well be… Well, you know."

I did.

Yet for some reason, I couldn't let the matter go. My head was already swimming a little, I'll admit, and Sig had refilled our glasses at some point during the conversation. "But you could save more lives by mending human-HoFeLaffian relations," I said. "Your people are dying on the streets every day."

"And that's my responsibility?" they said, slamming down their glass. Apparently, I had struck a nerve.

"No. Of course not. But preserving laffa—" I used their word without thinking— "is about more than just doing no harm." Something came over me, then, maybe it was the Holy Spirit, and I put my hand on theirs. "Our world must be saved, Sig. And you seem to always be the one to do the saving."

####

We talked about other things, too. How they loved our mountains. How they had not seen or heard from their father since he was taken into custody for questioning.

"I'm not trying to see or hear from him," they clarified. "I'd just like to know he's alive somewhere he can't cause more trouble."

"Understandable," I said. "You've all been through so much."

We talked more about laffa, and about my god, and a lot of other things I won't detail here. Then we went out into the garden and looked at my mother's garden, which Sig had revived. For the first time in years, I wanted to sketch—the moonlight on the faces of the snapdragons, the graves of the dug earth waiting for new seed, the criminal face of a scavenging racoon. It was a beautiful night, and one I would like to keep to myself, if the Council will allow it. All I can tell you is that I went to rest for a few hours in my childhood bed, and that, when I came down the next morning, Sig and the gin bottles were gone.

They took my car, by the way, which left me stranded there for a full day until police found it abandoned three towns over at a gas station pump and brought it back.

####

Despite how that night ended, our conversation changed me forever. I left the clergy and became a representative for human-HoFeLaffian relations. I was leader of the first Council for Peace for ten years. I adopted my HoFe son after the brutal murder of his parents.

But you know all of this, anyway, don't you?

You know that what I said to Sig ate and ate away at them, hiding in a cabin in the mountains.

You know because they eventually returned.

And I must say, it's a pleasure to see you again, General.

I'm glad you're back to save us.

ARTICLE TWENTY-FIVE

The Council

Official Order

September 1, 2160

The Council of HoFeLaffian Elders, chaired by General Sig, has heard from all witnesses in the matter of Humanity's atrocities against the people of Laffa and HoFe, as well as supporting documents provided by the prosecution and defense.

We have found these accounts alarming on all sides.

The politicians who initially called for this Council's investigation thirty years ago did so with the purpose of removing humans from Earth completely, whether by shipment to an alternate planet away from the HoFeLaffians or, in more extreme cases, genocide. The Council has not found a case for such extreme measures. Though humanity's crimes are by far the most atrocious, we must point out that the actions of the HoFeLaffa upon their takeover of Earth's governmental system also displayed a violence that betrayed the fundamental beliefs of this Council, and they cannot be ignored.

The human politicians have argued very effectively that the HoFeLaffa do not belong on Earth. The general public was not aware of the actions of HealthCorp on either planet, and the resulting takeover of Earth's governmental and economic systems by the displaced aliens was thus unjust. Such politicians call for the removal of the HoFeLaffa by way of the decommissioned HealthCorp star fleet, which has since been used for scientific research and is thus still operational.

Both sides have demonstrated, using a variety of persuasive charts and graphs, that, should they continue to stay on Earth, the HoFeLaffians will continue to lose their lives to hate crimes at an alarming rate.

The committee members have presented compelling evidence, and we have found ourselves agreeing, to various extents, with both of them.

As a result, have asked ourselves the most important question of all: How can we preserve laffa?

It is the decision of the Special Committee of Elders that the two groups cannot coexist in harmony. A new home must be found for the HoFeLaffians—but that home must be of suitable comfort and at no risk of environmental collapse.

We have finally decided to share our decision with the general public because such a planet has been discovered in galaxy 20,039. Much like Earth or Laffa, the planet is an appropriate mix of land and water. The biomes also include some areas of tropical rainforest reminiscent of the environment of HoFe. There is no indication that any major tectonic event will occur at any point in the near future—which, according to top scientists, means 10,000 years.

This decision has not been made lightly, and we understand that such a simplistic division of the blended population of Earth will prove problematic for families that consist of both human and HoFeLaffian individuals. In an additional gesture of peace and laffa, the HoFeLaffians have extended an invitation for all humans legally attached to HoFeLaffians—whether as spouses or adopted children—also be permitted to move to galaxy 20,039. We are sorry to report that the humans have not decided to uphold that gesture on their end, which means that no HoFeLaffians will be permitted to remain on Earth after the great departure, no matter the personal circumstances.

We hope, but do not expect, that one day both of our planets might again find peace.

In closing, the Council of HoFeLaffian Elders would like to thank both the HoFeLaffians and the humans for the privilege of our leadership over the last thirty years.

Long laffa.

EPILOGUE

Curator's Final Note

And so we come to the end of our journey together.

I'll admit that I took some liberties.

I'll admit that to an actual curator of human or HoFeLaffian history, my choices might seem overindulgent or even misleading.

But how else to capture the nuances of this great debate—the *greatest* debate, I might argue, in either of our species' histories—in just a short exhibit? How else to create the feeling that exists here, in the pit of my stomach, as I weigh the evidence and determine the outcome and feel, as the Council felt, that what is right and what is right for our people are two very different things?

An impossible task, indeed.

In a few hours, I will watch the fleet of ships exit Earth's atmosphere for the great unknown of galaxy 20,039. I will stand on my deck and hope that my documentation of this struggle will help future HoFeLaffians understand their past—where they came from, yes, but more importantly, *who they are*—to avoid repeating our mistakes in their future. I will hope, and I will watch, and then I will wait, for they will come for me, certainly, as soon as that last bright light disappears.

And at the very end, I will think of this song, known to our people for so many generations: *Laffa, long laffa. A gift, long laffa, a song, long laffa. We thank you, long laffa, and pass on long laffa.*

Laffa,

Laffa,

Laffa,

Laffa.

I will not keep you any longer, but will merely say long laffa to you, dear viewer, and to your children, who I hope will grow up in a better world than any we have seen.

Your most humble curator,

Joh

[Curator's Note: There will now be a blank screen and the sound of the endless ocean lapping at the hull of a boat so that those who wish to might say the fifty laffas for those who have been lost.]

Dr. Kelly Ann Jacobson is the author or editor of many published books, including her contest-winning chapbook *An Inventory of Abandoned Things* (Split/Lip Press), her award-winning young adult novel *Tink and Wendy* (Three Rooms Press), and her new young adult novel *Robin and Her Misfits* (Three Rooms Press). Kelly received her PhD in fiction from Florida State University and teaches creative writing full time as an Assistant Professor of English at the University of Lynchburg and as an instructor for Southern New Hampshire University's online MFA and Johns Hopkins University's MA in Writing. Kelly's short works have been published in such places as *Best Small Fictions, Boulevard, Southern Humanities Review, Daily Science Fiction,* and *Gargoyle.*

www.ingramcontent.com/pod-product-compliance
Lightning Source LLC
Chambersburg PA
CBHW061518020726
47502CB00006B/2131